Morelli and Larson Detective Agency:

Three New Cases

by Matthew Fearing

edited by

Dr. Kelly Bishop

BOOK 5 in the Buck Larson Adventures

This book is dedicated to Dr. Kelly Bishop who serves as the inspiration behind one of the main, recurring characters in the Buck Larson Adventure Series along with being my muse, sounding board and editor.

Additionally, dedication is to my youngest son, Henry, who inspires me to achieve as he survived being 3 months premature and now excels in mathematics and his mom, Christie, who shares in raising him toward manhood.

This book is a work of fiction. The characters are my creation. While I draw upon people I know for the inspiration and modeling of many of the characters, the people and situations are creations of mine and did not actually occur. Fun is in the fantasy and imagination which one can create with the mind.

Many of the places are real whether now existing or only existing in the past. The use of the places is to provide an anchor to both writer and the reader and are not intended as real depictions of the place or any event.

Morelli and Larson Detective Agency

Chapter 1: The Agency

Buck Larson looked at the new business cards that arrived in the mail. His partner, Dr. Kelley Morgan had picked out the design. A magnifying glass was the symbol and in bold print read **MORELLI & LARSON DETECTIVE AGENCY**. Half of the cards had Dr. Morgan's name imprinted below the business title, KELLEY M. MORGAN, Ph.D. Half of the cards had Buck Larson on them, BUCK LARSON. Each had Buck's home address in Eudora as their office. Dr. Morgan thought they should have Buchanan Larson on Buck's half, but Buchanan only went by Buck. He took pride in the new adventure. I know this because I am Buck Larson.

I had turned one of the first-floor rooms in my house into a small office in which to conduct business as the newly organized Morelli and Larson Detective Agency. Dr. Morgan, whose maiden name is Morelli, agreed to join with me in private investigation with she providing the analytical, and myself providing the investigative aspect. She also has a prior partnership as a psychologist with Dr. Danae Cornwall in Lawrence. Their administrative assistant, Tina Thomas, would also serve as the secretary for the detective agency with some additional pay. Kelley thought using Morelli as her name for the detective agency would help in keeping the two businesses separate and avoid potential confusion.

I first met Dr. Kelley Morgan as a referral patient to her following the death of my then girlfriend, a deputy sheriff from back in Posey County, Indiana. The connection between Kelley and myself was noticeable almost from the start. But with my luck in the romance field, the good doctor of course, was and is married, albeit not necessarily happily. Her husband, like all people, has some flaws. In his case, a couple major ones; but the two of them were working on it.

To add to the convoluted mess, my son, Theodore - who I call Teddy - and her daughter, Charlotte - who everyone calls Charlie - were dating. The two were a cute couple and quite infatuated with each other. But then, why wouldn't they be? Teddy was a lot like me, and Charlie was a lot like her mother, beautiful and smart.

Yet, through it all, Kelley and I discovered that we do make a good team.

We just had to resist the temptation of each other, knowing that it wouldn't be morally right. We acknowledged the desire and connection which helped in the fight to not do wrong.

The whole idea of a detective agency came about through being frequently called upon to work with law enforcement in solving crimes. From working with the local, small town police force to helping with the FBI, I seemed to be called upon to use my talents and experiences in particularly tough cases. It was suggested to me by one FBI agent, Delores, that I might as well get into the business and charge for my services. I did have a knack for getting to the bottom of cases and not over-reacting to the situations. With that, the first detective agency in Eudora, Kansas was set up in my house just off Pilla Park on the north edge of town.

Eudora rests aside the Wakarusa River, just five miles east of Lawrence with around 7000 residents. A few restaurants, a grocery store, and a whole lot of churches are part of the town's make-up. Small businesses with a personal appeal dot the Eudora landscape. An accountant, a plumber, a little boutique, along with chiropractic services are in town without rhyme or reason where they are other than the owner likes Eudora and that is what they do. For that very reason, the Morelli and Larson Detective Agency is in Eudora. The advantage of being not too far from the college town that hosts the University of Kansas or from the Kansas City metropolitan area certainly doesn't hurt. Even Topeka is not too far.

My reputation didn't hurt either in setting up the business. The work with the FBI in a couple cases had brought about some publicity that exaggerated my prowess as an investigator. I also headed up a charitable foundation in southwestern Indiana which helped the people in and around Posey County and particularly Mount Vernon. The media loves to make out heroes solving crimes and doing good. Personally, if I could, I'd just get on my Harley and ride. Go wherever it felt good to go and then ride some more. But there were obligations. To my son. To my friends. To people I loved and had loved. The detective agency gave me enough freedom to choose what I wanted to do - within reason - while providing me a job. A jog that allowed me to work with someone I very much cared about. I ended up in one case or another anyway; might as well make it a paying job.

My phone started buzzing. Ed Hatfield, Eudora's Chief of Police and my good friend was calling. "Hello, Ed."

"Buck! Just thought I'd call and see how your new venture was going."

"No cases yet unless you're looking to throw something my way."

"Knock on wood, things have been quiet since that little chase you were on with the FBI. Besides, I'm not sure we can afford your fees now that you've gone official."

"I'm sure I could work out a friend's discount for you." I laughed.

"I'll take the quiet. Erin wants me to invite you over to dinner tonight." Erin Hatfield, Ed's wife, was also a good friend.

"Sure. Steaks on the grill?"

"Don't I always?"

"I'll bring the wine."

"See you later then."

Over the years, I had been going over to Ed's house many times. Ed always grilled steaks and I always brought the wine. It had become a bit of a tradition.

With nothing else to do, I decided to hop on the Harley and go for a ride. I went down to the basement garage and wiped down the old 1958 Harley Duo-Glide with a bit of pride. The bike and I had been through a lot together. The green and white two-tone paint scheme. The S&S replacement engine to give the bike more power. The classic styling with genuine leather saddle bags. I had picked up the bike when a young man from a farmer that I had worked for.

Pulling her out of the garage, I went up to Casey's to top off my tank. Along with some gas, I picked up some lottery tickets. It wasn't that I needed the money. I just seemed to have luck in that area. I didn't consider myself rich, but I had enough. Ironic that I was lucky in an area that, for the most part, I was frugal, and yet so unlucky in romance. Something always seemed to happen in my love life; divorce, already married, new job, and even death conspired against my having a good, lasting relationship. Money seemed to find its way to me. But like they say - and like the Beatles sang - money can't buy me love.

I pulled out and headed west out 10th Street. The sun felt nice as I glided down the Eudora Flats toward Lawrence enjoying the slow climb toward the city. I could see buildings on the University of Kansas campus, high up on the hill in the center of town. I cut through Lawrence using 6th Street to get to the west side of town. The town was growing with expansion continuing on out as both the city and the university reached out for more space.

I passed the Christmas tree farm just outside of town and over to Stull Road. I turned left to take that road and headed toward Topeka down the winding little highway. Winter was giving way to Spring and little buds were starting to show on the trees. I was careful to watch for slick spots in the shade under the trees. Beyond Shawnee Heights, the golf courses at Lake Shawnee were starting to fill with people trying their best to knock little white balls into small little holes in the ground. I golfed occasionally, but the reality was that I am an awful golfer. I was even a dangerous one. I never knew where the ball was going when I hit it, but I did hit it hard.

Eventually I reached Topeka Boulevard and I turned north. South would have given me a more rural ride, but I wanted to stop at the Harley shop in Topeka that sat along Topeka Boulevard. In addition to selling and servicing Harleys, the shop had a very nice little museum and a renowned barbecue restaurant in the building. My HOG (Harley Owners Group) group, the Oz Chapter, was based there.

I pulled into the parking lot and checked my phone. There was a voice message from James Gilliford. He was an attorney and the fiancé of my partner Kelley's other business partner, Danae Cornwall. While we knew each other - we were more acquaintances than friends - James and I were not in the habit of calling each other. The message asked me to call him when I got a chance and that it had to do with my new enterprise. I decided to call him back after I got back home from my ride. I wasn't being rude. I might need to take some notes from the call.

I cut my visit to the Harley shop short and headed north out of Topeka, catching U.S. 24 and heading back east to Lawrence. Driving through Perry, I decided to bypass Lawrence proper and continue down U.S. 24 toward the airport, cutting over on Kansas 32 to get back to Eudora.

My house sits to the north of town, just on the other side of the railroad tracks. The hill to downtown had my house toward the base of the rise. I pulled the bike into the garage and then wiped her down. I pondered getting a farm-style fuel tank so I could just fill up the bike there at the house. Eudora didn't have a lot of restrictions, but I wasn't sure where they would stand on a 200-gallon fuel tank sitting up in my backyard. Somehow, I thought it might be frowned upon.

I gave Gilliford a return call. "James, what can I do for you?"

"I have a client who could use your services. Her husband went missing. Can you come into my office and talk about this case?"

"I'll be there in about an hour. Will that do?"

"Perfect."

I hung up. Morelli and Larson Detective Agency looked like it was getting its first case. I gave Kelley a call and we agreed that I'd get the initial information and then I'd get back with her. She was excited about this start to our business.

The Case of the Missing Husband

Chapter 2: Missing You

James Gilliford's office was out on Wakarusa Drive in west Lawrence. I pulled the Harley back out of the garage and checked the oil. Old Harley's can sometimes go through some oil, but the Duo-Glide was doing fine. I wiped down the bike and gave her a pat before kicking her back to life. The kick starter went smoothly, but then the bike had been running not that long ago.

I headed out of Eudora and rolled onto K-10, staying on it until I got to the stoplight by the Clinton Park ballfields. I turned toward Wakarusa heading north, eventually pulling into the parking lot of the bank of businesses that included Mr. Gilliford's office. The Harley stood in stark contrast to the high-dollar, luxury cars in the lot. I remembered a female friend saying to her girlfriend to not be fooled by Harley riders' clothes. Those guys that have Harleys have some money she told her. The problem, she continued, is that they spend it all on their bikes. Very often, this was true.

Once inside the office, the receptionist looked up. The 6'4" frame of a man wearing a black leather jacket and blue jeans brought about a look of disdain from the grey haired, spectacled lady.

"May I help you?" Her tone bordered on snooty.

"Mr. Gilliford asked me to come in to see him."

"You're …?" She left the sentence hanging.

"Mr. Larson."

She looked at her calendar and then back up at me. "I'm sorry, he doesn't have an appointment listed with a Mr. Larson."

I sat down. "I'll wait then."

The lady looked at a loss. She picked up the phone and called in to her boss, James Gilliford. She tried to keep it a whisper but in the quiet office, it was easy to hear anyway. After a brief minute, Mr. Gilliford stepped out.

"Buck! Hey, thanks for coming. Come on in." He gestured for me to go into his private office.

The secretary looked at me and shook her head while frowning. I took it that Mr. Gilliford generally dealt with well-dressed, high class clients.

"Please excuse, Peggy. She can be a bit proper."

"Proper isn't the word I was thinking of."

Gilliford laughed. "No, I guess most people wouldn't after meeting her. But she is quite efficient."

"So, James," I wasn't sure exactly what to call him really, "what do you have for me?"

"A missing husband. Guy's name is Tony Johnston. Well, he was born Anthony Johnston. His wife, Carla Pence Johnston, reported his missing status to the police after he didn't come home late last week, but they haven't come up with anything."

"Where was he last seen?"

"He went to work at his office last Friday, but no one is sure when he left or recall seeing him go. They have flexible office hours so people can come and go as long as they get their time in and get the job done."

"No foul play suspected?"

"Not by the police. They say he just kind of left the grid. There is nothing to indicate violence."

"Any insurance on him?"

"There is life insurance, but it would take a death certificate or death notice for the wife to collect. Nothing else we are aware of anyway."

"I take it the wife is your client?"

"Yes. Well, they both have been."

"Do you have any theories?"

"Not really. He just seemed to disappear. Don't think there was anyone who would want to get rid of him. It seems like he just went 'poof' and was gone. I can't imagine why. He and his wife are average people who don't really get involved in much. Families are well-to-do, but Tony and Carla are upper middle class. Nothing extravagant."

"Where's his office?"

"He worked from home sometimes and went to the main office in Topeka sometimes depending on what needed to be done. Do you think you can follow this up for my client?"

"I can try."

Gilliford slid a contract over to me stipulating the daily pay and acceptable incidentals that could be charged. I gave it a brief look. There was one-month limit to the investigation.

I looked at Gilliford questioningly. "Is there a specific reason for the one-month limit?"

"No event. It's just that would pretty much stretch Mrs. Johnston's finances. The families don't seem willing to help; not even his parents. I guess he has been a bit of a disappointment to both families."

"Not a problem. Let's work on getting the situation resolved and hopefully it won't take even a month."

"I know Mrs. Johnston would appreciate that. She just wants to know where he is and what happened to him."

I signed the contract knowing that the attorney needed it for his file. I took down a few notes and got the home address for the Johnstons as well as the work address in Topeka.

Peggy did not look up as I came out of the office. I'm sure she was a wonderful gatekeeper for Mr. Gilliford and appreciated by his clients. I mused that she would make an excellent librarian of old. Or maybe better, a Marine drill sergeant.

My next stop would be the Lawrence Police Department to pick up a copy of and get information from the missing person report. The west branch of the police department was just off Wakarusa on 15th Street not far from Gilliford's office. I pulled into the lot and saw a small group that rode with the Blue Angels, a law enforcement-based motorcycle group. I had ridden with the guys down to Williamsburg, Kansas for some barbecue a previous summer.

"Still riding that old motorcycle?" one of the guy's called out. "Don't you think you ought to trade it in for something that actually runs?"

One thing about cops. You are going to get teased. You know you are really in trouble when they are being straight serious with you. I smiled and took my ribbing. I doubted any of them knew I had opened a detective agency. It usually took a bit to get friendly cooperation as a private detective. It was too often perceived that if you, the private detective could solve the case when the police didn't, you made them look bad.

Fortunately, a missing person case wouldn't cause too much concern unless it was rather high profile or the detective got too critical of the police effort.

The desk sergeant took my request and after a bit of waiting, a lieutenant came out with a folder and beckoned me back to an office.

"Not much to go on, I'm afraid. Guy showed up to work in Topeka and then just never goes home. Wife made report here in Lawrence. Left his car there in the lot. Nothing. It's like he wanted to disappear."

"What kind of car did he have, Lieutenant?"

"Hmmm, looks like he had an older Buick Skylark. Kansas license MZB-012. Topeka dusted it for prints. His were on the steering wheel and dash. Wife's on the passenger side dash and door. That's it."

"Sounds like he just walked off and didn't look back."

"That's what I'm thinking. Got tired of it all and just walked. Maybe hitch-hiked somewhere. We had an alert out through the Kansas Highway Patrol for 48 hours, but no leads. Good-luck, Mr. Larson."

"Thanks."

I headed out the door and back to my bike which had even more admiring officers around it. I never minded my bike getting the admiration that it deserved, and we all chatted about the bike for a bit before I could get away.

My next stop was Kelley's downtown office on Massachusetts Street. I headed down 15th Street and cut over and through the KU campus up on the hill. Coming down the hill, I passed The Wheel, a favorite bar for KU students. The parking garage off New Hampshire Street was where Kelley usually parked and as I pulled in, I could see her Jaguar not far from the motorcycle parking area. She was at least in her office, but likely had a client.

"Well, Good Morning Mr. Larson," Tina greeted. Tina Thomas was the always cheerful administrative assistant who worked for both the counseling offices of Drs. Morgan and Cornwall as well as the detective agency of Morelli and Larson.

"Good Morning, Tina. It's a pleasure to see you."

Tina beamed. "Dr. Morgan is just about to finish with a patient. Do you mind waiting?"

"Not at all. How did you know I was here to see her?"

"Mr. Larson! Who else would you be here to see?"

"Maybe I came to see you."

Tina blushed. "You would have just called if you needed me."

"I need to stop being so predictable."

Tina laughed as the door opened to Kelley's office. A man walked out timidly.

"We can talk more about it next session," Kelley told the man. He nodded and left. Kelley looked at me. "Come on in."

I stepped into her office. Kelley went back to sit at her desk turning to face me. Once she sat down, I started.

"Danae's boyfriend is sending us this one. It's a missing person case; a husband who seems to have just vanished."

"I assume she made a police report. What did they have to say?"

"Basically, they don't have any reason to believe foul play. He just seems to have disappeared. His car was left at his work. He arrived at work, but no one seems to remember him even leaving. Doesn't sound like he was close to many, if any, of his colleagues."

"What about his wife? Did they get along?"

"There were no reports of problems. I haven't talked to the wife yet. Thought we might talk to her together so I can get your perspective and insight."

"Sounds good. My first impression is that he just wanted to disappear. How hard would that be to do?"

"I would think it would be harder than most people imagine. Credit card trails. Use of bank accounts. Something would likely show up. Toll readers. I.D. checks."

"So, if he wanted to disappear, it would have to be fairly well planned out."

"Yes. Patience and planning." Did this guy plan out his disappearance? Was he nabbed? It could be a case of mistaken identity and then he couldn't be released because it would give away the plan. The police didn't seem to think it was foul play. If he had been kidnapped at work, certainly someone would have seen him leaving. And what about street or security cameras?

Kelley checked her calendar. She had no other patients for the afternoon. She was free to go.

"Do you want to ride with me or should we go separately? I'm guessing you rode your Harley."

"You know it. I'll ride with you."

"Tina, would you let Danae know I'm out with Buck on a case?"

"Of course," replied Tina. "How exciting! Your first detective case."

Kelley and I smiled. It was our first case together.

Chapter 3: The Worried Wife

Carla Pence Johnston was a moderately attractive woman. She wouldn't win any beauty pageants, but she would turn a few heads of the men her age. She had a pleasant voice.

"Come in." Mrs. Johnston greeted us at the door. "Mr. Gilliford let me know you had taken the case for me."

"Thank you, Mrs. Johnston. This is my colleague, Dr. Morgan."

"Please, just call me Kelley." Kelley stuck out her hand to take Mrs. Johnston's hand. She didn't really shake it. She held it in a sympathetic gesture. One could see Mrs. Johnston relax a bit then.

"Oh, and call me Carla." Mrs. Johnston indicated the living room. "Won't you please sit down?" The house was very well kept and tidy.

I waited for Mrs. Johnston to sit down, too. "Could you tell us when you became worried about your husband going missing?"

"Well, he's very erratic about the times he gets home when he goes into the office. I wasn't really worried until it got to be time for bed. He is very religious about bedtime."

"Did he go into the office often?" Kelley asked.

"Oh, he hated going to Topeka, but he's been going in more over the last few months. He said that they needed him to do work there to help with some new employees."

Kelley followed up. "Did he have a lot of friends among his co-workers?"

"I don't think so. He never mentioned anyone and no one from the company called except when there was some work they needed him to do. He's not a very social type. None of his co-workers ever came over to the house."

I was trying to get a better idea of Mr. Johnston. "What did he do for fun?"

"Fun? That's not something I ever associated with Tony."

"Well, what drew you to him? What was it about him that led you to marry him?"

"Honestly, it was more of a family expectation. I guess neither of us measured up to family expectations. I think our parents were expecting an heir, probably the most they hoped from us. Unfortunately, I can't have children. That didn't really seem to bother Tony, though."

Kelley jumped back in. "Do you have friends you talk to or do anything with?"

"Not really. I like staying to myself. I read and keep house; cleaning and cooking. I like to think I'm a good cook."

"Your house looks nice - very well maintained."

"Thank you. Tony doesn't really notice unless it starts getting messy and he's not a picky eater."

"How does he let you know he thinks it's messy?" I asked.

"Actually, he would ask if I'm feeling okay. He is used to me keeping everything up unless I'm sick. He doesn't yell or anything, but he doesn't help out either. He says home is my responsibility and the outside the house and making money is his."

Kelley interjected. "Kind of old-fashioned thinking."

"It's how our families think it should be." Carla shrugged.

I wanted to get back to the day he went missing. "Did he say or do anything unusually on the day or days before he went missing?"

"Not really. He seemed a bit more distant than usual. Maybe a bit more preoccupied, but that may be me projecting. He was never very attentive."

"Did he go anywhere other than work?"

"He sometimes went out to work in the evening. Sometimes he said he just needed some fresh air to take a break from work."

"Did you ever go with him when he took a break?"

"No. The one time I asked him if he needed company, he made seem to be an imposition; he said he just needed to be alone a bit."

"Do you know where he went?"

"No. Just out. He'd be gone for a few hours. I figured he found somewhere to walk around."

Kelley looked at me. I nodded. About enough time to see someone else.

"Did he use a cell phone?" I asked.

"Yes, of course. I called his phone when I started worrying that he hadn't come home. It kept going to voice mail."

"Did anyone find his phone?"

"It was left on his desk. I have it now. There are no messages or call history on it. It seems to be blank."

"Can I see it?"

Mrs. Johnston handed me the phone. I turned it on and went to the call log. It had been cleared. I then looked at the blocked numbers. There were 5 blocked numbers.

I handed the phone back to Mrs. Johnston. "Do you recognize any of those blocked numbers"

She looked at the phone screen. "No. But I don't pay attention to numbers after I log them into a phone."

Four of the phone numbers had a local area code. I noted the block numbers.

"Is there anything else you can think of that might help us find Tony?"

"I told the police everything I know. Our families are here in the area. I just don't know what else there might be. I almost expected a ransom note, but we don't really have much money. Our parents are slightly well off, but their money is all tied up in investments and business. It wouldn't be available."

"The police don't seem to think there is foul play. They agree that it doesn't appear to be a kidnapping."

Kelley backed up what I was saying. "I don't think it's a kidnapping either. Maybe something happened. Has he been sick or been to a doctor lately?"

Mrs. Johnston thought for a moment. "I don't think so. He doesn't like going to doctors. I think he only got a physical about 5 years ago because the company he works for required it for their insurance."

I looked over at Kelley. "A bump on the head? Amnesia?"

"That's rather rare, but I suppose it is possible. It would be more likely triggered by an event or strong memory. Something traumatic."

Kelley and I looked at Mrs. Johnston for any kind of confirmation. She shook her head no.

"What about your finances?" I asked. "I hope you don't mind me asking?" I added.

"We seem to be doing fine. Of course, we have the mortgage on this house. There are only a couple more payments on my car and his was paid for. We belong to the country club, but that's because both of our families belong and they expect us to remain members. Generally, they pay for our membership - a gift each year - and then we occasionally go up for dinner or play some golf. Of course, I don't handle the finances. He did."

I nodded. "Might he have had a gambling problem?" I glanced over at Kelley. She didn't react which was good. I know that gambling was one of the problems she had with her own husband. He was attending Gamblers Anonymous to deal with the issue.

"No. I think I'd have known. But then again, I didn't think he'd just up and leave either. But if he didn't get taken, I don't know what to think."

"Well, Ma'am," I looked over what I had, "I'm going to follow up on a couple things and we'll get back with you or your attorney."

"Thank you."

Mrs. Johnston walked us to the door. As soon as we left, she shut and locked the door.

"She seems kind of strange," Kelley said as we got into her car.

"Yes, but I think that is the natural state for her. She seems the perfect fit for the Tony Johnston that is coming to light."

"Maybe. What leads are we following now?"

"The blocked numbers were blocked recently. I'd like to know what they are. Could be hiding something."

"What about cameras?"

"That would be a lot to go through. No one knows when he left and there are hundreds of people in his building, let alone the thousands walking by in Topeka. It is something we could get back to if there is nothing else."

"Monitor bank activity?"

"It's been dead, but we can check with Gilliford to make sure an alert is given if it's used. I would guess that the police already asked them to do that, but doesn't hurt to follow up."

"I'll call James on that while you check the phone. I can do that from my office."

Kelley had pulled into the garage and parked in about the same spot.

"Sounds good, partner."

We both smiled at hearing the word partner. Kelley waved and headed inside to her office. I jumped on my Harley and headed out to my home office. No one can just disappear. Could they?

That evening, I got a fire going in the chiminea on the deck just off the kitchen. I had invited Ed and Erin Hatfield to come by and have a beer. I asked Kelley if she could come out so we could casually update the status of the case.

"Buck," Kelley started, "Charlie wants to know if she can come out, too. Teddy is coming by to pick her up and she told him she'd love to come out and be with us. Can you believe it?! My teenage daughter wants to hang out with her mom!"

"I can believe it. They're good kids. Teddy had already called to let me know he was dropping by."

"They both seem to be very mature in dating each other. It's not all goo-goo eyes and the typical teenage romance."

"Well, college is right around the corner. That will be an interesting time."

"They talk about where they want to go quite a bit. I think they are planning on going to the same college."

"Right now, the talk is of North Carolina. Is that what Charlie is thinking?"

"She is, but she's keeping her options open. They've talked about Kansas, Tulane, North Dakota, and Evansville."

"Hmmm, Evansville is new in the mix. Why Evansville?"

"I guess some of the programs are top-notch. Time is coming up where they will have to make a decision."

"That's true. We will see soon. Did you get ahold of Gilliford about the bank activity?"

"Yes. He already has an alert set up for the account. He had Mrs. Johnston authorize it for the police. Nothing so far. What about the blocked numbers?"

"I think I've got something. I'll tell you more about it when you get out here. Ed and Erin just arrived."

"Okay, see you soon. I think Teddy and Charlie will be there is just a bit."

I hung up just as Teddy pulled up in his old, red Plymouth Valiant. Both he and Charlie were giggling and laughing as they got out of the car. They used the gate rather than going through the house.

"Hey, Dad!"

"Hi, Son. Hello, Charlie."

"Hello, Mr. Larson. How are you doing?"

"Fine. Your mom is just heading out."

Charlie and Teddy headed over by the fire. There was a slight chill in the air; more cool than cold.

"How's the Valiant holding up?" Ed asked Teddy.

"It's great. I love it. I can't thank your sister enough for letting me have it."

"Believe me, Teddy, she is delighted that you have it."

Erin got up. She felt comfortable playing hostess at my house. I would never ask her to do that, but we were all like family. She grabbed a plate of cheese, meat and crackers that I had prepared for us to snack on.

"You kids want something to drink?" she asked the young couple.

"Whatever you have," answered Charlie. Teddy nodded.

Along with the plate, Erin brought out a Ski soda for each of the kids. I usually picked up some of the regional soda when I was back in the Evansville area. It had a unique lemon-lime and orange taste. Both Teddy and Charlie had developed a taste for it.

I reached into the cooler and pulled out a Sterling beer. Ed indicated he was ready for one, so I tossed him one. I looked up at Erin and she nodded. I opened one and handed it to her.

Ed kicked back in his chair. "So how's your first official detective agency case going? Missing person, isn't it?"

"It's interesting. The guy just seems to have disappeared. Car left at work. No credit card or bank activity. But I did find something interesting, I think, in his phone."

Kelley pulled up right about that time. We all waved for her to come through the gate. She smiled and waved.

Charlie gave her mom a hug as she came up onto the deck, and I handed her a can of Sterling.

"You still have some of this stuff?" She laughed. "Are you having someone ship it to you?"

"Actually, I do. They send me a case a month. Standard order. Comes straight from the Louisville plant."

"Where's Patrick this evening?" Erin asked.

"Oh, he and Victor are playing in an e-league. They have a Fortnite match this evening. I don't think they even noticed I had left." Kelley took a sip of the beer and turned to me. "So, what's up with the blocked calls?"

"Well, to me it lends credibility to the idea he planned to leave. There were a few numbers blocked just before he went missing. One in particular looked interesting. There is a history of a lot of calls from that number. I called and made arrangements to meet with the person tomorrow at 10:00 a.m." I took a sip of my beer. "Kelley, I'm hoping you can make it at that time."

"I can. At least for a bit. Who is the person?

"She is an Aimee Flynn."

"She?"

"Yes, and they've been calling and texting each other for months now. Two of the four other numbers are her work and her house number."

The little party went on for another couple of hours. Teddy left with Charlies after about an hour. Kelley left about a half-hour after the kids left. I walked her out to the car, excusing myself for a moment from Ed and Erin.

"This case is getting interesting, Buck."

"It sure is taking a path I hadn't expected."

"So what about our kids? Are you guiding Teddy toward any particular college?"

"No, and as you well know, I think the two of them will pick the same college. They're both bright, so I don't worry too much about the quality of education. I just hope they play everything smart. They seem to be."

"I think so, too. Charlie is leaning toward the University of North Carolina. We are thinking about a trip out this summer to see the college. Maybe even get a family vacation in. Are you going to head that way?"

"I might take Teddy out. You know his mom's family stay out in Wilmington, North Carolina for part of the year. If I take him out to see the campus, I can drive the little bit farther to Wilmington. Maybe we can time it so the kids will be out there at the same time."

"That would put us out there at the same time." She winked.

"Hmmm, I guess it would."

Kelley laughed. "We can talk about it more, later. See you at the office tomorrow before 10."

I nodded and shut the car door as she got in. She took off and I went back to talk with Ed and Erin.

“You’ve sure got it bad for that girl,” Erin remarked.

“I’ve never denied it.”

Ed grinned. “Buck, you end up in some interesting situations.”

We cleaned up and continued chatting. Erin gave me a big hug as she and Ed left. They were definitely good friends. They were family.

Chapter 4: The Other Woman

I was at Kelley's office at 9:30. She was already set to go. I think she was getting excited about detective work which seemed a little strange to me. As a psychologist, she did plenty of detective work of the mind. And she was good at it. That was part of the reason I wanted to partner with her in the detective agency. Her enthusiasm was contagious, and I found myself getting energized about the case. Of course, the other part was that I simply enjoyed being around her.

"Buck, do you think the man we've heard described to us has a girlfriend on the side?"

"Well, I agree that the man we had depicted for us seems quite different from the playboy who would have a girlfriend, but that split personality may explain the disappearance."

"But she's allowing us to come over which implies, I would think, that he isn't with her right now."

"True, but let's see what she has to say. She could be trying to knock us off the trail."

The address led to a very small house in east Lawrence. We had passed a large cemetery before turning on her street. The house was still nice. The yard was maintained with a nice yard of grass and trimmed bushes.

I knocked on the door and a blond-haired lady answered. She wore sweatpants and a t-shirt. I guessed she had just been working out.

"Come in. I assume you are Mr. Larson."

"Thank you. This is my partner, Dr. Morgan."

"Doctor? Are you two like that one detective? Umm, Sherlock Holmes?"

I laughed. "I suppose, although I hadn't really thought of us as Holmes and Watson before."

Kelley shook her head, but smiled.

We sat down in her small living room. It was modestly furnished.

"Can I get you some coffee?" asked Miss Flynn.

"Thank you, I rarely turn down coffee," I answered.

"None for me. Thanks." Kelley added, "Would you like me to help, though?"

"That would be sweet."

The two ladies went into the kitchen. Now I felt a little awkward left in the front room by myself. I heard light laughter and started to get up to join them, but I imagined Kelley was bonding a little with her and I didn't want to interfere with that. They came back in with Aimee holding one cup of coffee and Kelley holding one for me. She held it out to me to take and winked. She had made a connection.

"Aimee tells me that she and Tony have been seeing each other for about four months." Kelley looked over to Aimee for confirmation. Aimee nodded. "But all of a sudden recently, she couldn't get ahold of him. He stopped answering his phone and her calls were blocked."

"Did he give you a reason for not wanting to see you anymore?" I asked.

Aimee lowered her head. "I told him I was pregnant with his kid. At first, he seemed to be okay with the baby, but that only lasted about a week."

Kelley patted her hand sympathetically. "Did you expect anything from him? Support or help?"

"I told him I was excited to have the baby and talked about how we could raise the child. I knew he was married. Stupid of me. Of course, he talked about how awful his wife was and how he would eventually leave her. But I'm no dummy. I know men say those things to make it seem okay that they're fooling around. And of course, I accepted it to make it okay that I was fooling around with him."

"I don't want to sound indelicate, but are you sure the baby is his and, I guess more importantly, was he sure it was his?" I had asked it. Kelley made a face at me, but it had to be asked.

"I understand. The baby is definitely his. I haven't been with another man for a few years now. He knew that as well. He never asked me if it could have been someone else's baby."

"So, did you discuss support?"

"I told him that if he wasn't leaving his wife, I'd at least need him to help with raising the baby. I refuse to get an abortion. I didn't care if he helped secretly or openly, but that I couldn't afford to do this on my own."

"Did he suggest an abortion?" Kelley asked.

"No. Initially he was just going to help me raise the baby. Something about setting up an allotment. Like I said, I knew deep down he wasn't going to leave his wife. Then when he refused to answer my calls; well, I was about to go see about an attorney. Then Mr. Larson called and said he wanted to talk to me about him being missing." She looked directly at me. "Do you think something happened to him? Do you think his wife found out and got rid of him?"

"Well, I know he is missing. I don't think his wife knew about you. But people can be kind of sneaky. Kelley and I will be doing our best to find him."

"I don't know what I hope. If he just skipped out on me and the baby, I hope he goes to hell. But I don't want something violent to have happened to him."

Kelley nodded. "I get it. I understand."

"Would you let us know if you do hear from him?" I handed Aimee one of our cards. She looked at it and nodded.

As we walked out, Aimee called out to us. "If you find him, will you at least let me know that you did? Find him that is."

"Of course," Kelley replied. I frowned at her. I knew she wanted to do the right thing, but I worried that we may not be able to and our first concern had to be our own client.

We got into Kelley's car and headed back to her office. She looked over at me.

"I guess I shouldn't have told her we would let her know if we find him."

"Probably not. It might be out of our control. But, I suspect if we find him, you'll be able to tell her. Let's not worry about that now."

"So do you think he left town because of the baby?"

"I think it might have something to do with it."

"It's like he lived a double life. Not just two lives, but two totally different lives."

"How so?"

"He seems to have grown up and married while he was this milk toast kind of guy. It turns out he's been fooling around and living this playboy kind of style."

"Maybe something compelled him to snap out of his 'milk toast' existence."

"We still haven't got a line on where he might be."

Kelley parked the car near her office. She turned to look at me. I assumed she was curious what I was thinking.

"Well, we now know that he had a girlfriend on the side and we don't think she knows where he is since he has seemed to have abandoned her, too."

"A girlfriend that is pregnant with his child."

"That might make him run. He might be afraid his family would really cut him out, but on the other hand, they don't seem to be doing too much for him anyway. Maybe he thought they eventually would."

"He could have gotten tired of just doing what the family expected of him or feeling like he's disappointed the family."

"We know that he had to plan something like this. You can't just escape like he has on a whim. It would take money and some timing."

"Where would you go if you were trying to escape everything, Buck?"

"Well, flying would leave a trace of where I left from and where I was going. At least if I flew from the United States. Even if I could fly my own plane, there would be some tracking."

"So you have to go by ground or sea."

"Sailing would be possible if you had your own boat, but they still track ships going out and coming in most places. It is a possibility. By ground would limit one to Canada or Mexico from here.

Canada is a possibility, but it's a limited one. Mexico would be easier to get into without too much scrutiny. Getting back into the U.S. would be tough, but getting out wouldn't be that hard. I guess I'd go to Mexico to disappear. But while a lot of people speak English along the border, it is a Spanish-speaking country."

"But whether Mexico or Canada, you'd still have to have money. I think that might be our key. If he's not using his accounts now, what is he using? Even with advanced planning, it would be obvious if he had siphoned off very much money."

"Yes, and he isn't working at a place he could steal money from. Maybe he won big at a casino? I've known some people who have done well at casinos."

Kelley laughed at me. I had won big money at a casino down in Puerto Rico by mistaking $1000 chits as $100 chits. I was fortunate that the error and gambling had been in my favor.

"How he is getting money is key to solving this, Buck."

"I think you're right. I'm going to look at a few possibilities. I might get lucky."

We got out of Kelley's Jaguar. She gave me a hug.

"This is exciting, Buck."

I smiled and then walked over to my old Harley. "It is, isn't it?"

Kelley headed up to her office upstairs and I motored off toward Eudora. I needed to look into a few things.

Once back home, I gave James Gilliford a call.

"Good afternoon, Buck. Any updates?"

"Well, first of all, Tony had a girlfriend and she's pregnant."

"Wow! Never would have guessed that. Is he with her?"

"No. He skipped out on her as well. Her pregnancy may have been the trigger, but I don't know for sure."

"I could imagine it would be. Any idea where he might have gone?"

"Looking into it. Have you looked into his tax records?"

"Umm, not recently. Why?"

"We've got his bank accounts - the ones we know about - and his credit cards covered, but he has to have some money. I'm curious if there have been any reported income or recently paid taxes."

"I can submit a request for records due to his current status and per his wife."

"Sounds good. How long do you think it will take?"

"Usually would take some time, but I can see about expediting it."

"Thanks. I think this might tell us something."

I started looking through the internet for big gambling type wins. Maybe a big casino win. Those would often be advertised though. Kansas City has casinos on both sides of the state line. Topeka has a few casinos on Native American land north of Topeka, but hitting it real big would be news. Oklahoma has casinos, but there is no indication that he had been down around that area.

The state lottery had Power Ball and Mega Millions that were high dollar games if you won. Kansas does allow the winner to remain anonymous. There were other games, too that might add up to significant dollars. I looked at the last few months of winners. There was a Mega Million winner whose name was not revealed that had won in Kansas. Missouri makes the winner's name public. Could it be that Tony had won the Mega Millions?

I decided to wait until I heard back from James before saying anything to anyone else. It almost seemed impossible odds, but somebody wins eventually. What would most people do if they hit it big? And if they didn't have to let on that they were the winner? And if they got their girlfriend pregnant while they were married?

Gilliford called back in the afternoon.

"Well, Sir, your instincts seem to be top notch."

"He hit the lottery, didn't he?" I was sure of it now.

"Wow! Right on. Of course, the lottery doesn't release the name of winners without permission, but he had to pay the taxes on his winnings."

"Any chance they let you know where the funds were deposited from the lottery winnings?"

"Working on it. Since his wife technically should receive half the winnings, I have contacted the lottery office to ascertain where the money was sent. I may have to file a motion in court to get the information. A formality."

"I'll bet he has an off-shore account. Still may be hard to trace him, but not impossible."

"Assuming the money is still in the account transferred to, we should be able to get information since they'd have to agree to certain restrictions before receiving the funds."

"Once you get that information, I can do the follow up. I think we are getting closer."

"I do, too. I'll let Mrs. Johnston know the progress being made."

I hung up and called Kelley to let her know where we stood in the investigation. We now knew what "triggered" his leaving. After talking to Kelley, I planned to call the police to give them an update. The closest we would have to any criminal activity would be the failure to split funds with his wife. Since it is more of a domestic issue, it would probably be dropped by the police. It would be a civil matter. Even the taxes got paid.

"So, even with that," Kelley asked, "how do we find him?"

"I think we will be able to get his address, or at least narrow it down, from the bank. Right now I'm thinking Mexico, but Belize would be a real possibility. They speak English there."

"Used to be called British Honduras, didn't it?"

"You are up on your geographic history."

"I'm more than just a pretty face, Buck."

"But you certainly have a very pretty face."

"You! Stop flirting and let me know what I can do."

"I think that once we have the information, a visit to Mr. Johnston will be in order. There really isn't any criminal activity so a lot of this may be for naught."

"Well, we are just being paid to find him. I guess it will be up to lawyers and diplomats after that."

"That's very true. There is only so much we can do."

"I have a client coming in. Talk to you later."

I hung up and called the Lawrence Police Department. After getting switched over to the officer who took the case originally, he took down the information and asked if I wouldn't mind giving him a copy of my report when I was done. I told him I didn't think the client would mind, but I'd have to check with her. It was something I knew that they would be pleased to have off their books.

James Gilliford got back with me during the evening. He was excited.

"The Kansas Lottery was able to provide the bank information since the wife was due half and didn't receive. He is using a bank in Saint Lucia."

"That's great."

"Well, I'm not done. If we bring down a letter of explanation from me, in my legal capacity, they will consider providing information on the account."

"You going down there?"

"Well, by we, I mean you."

I laughed. "I'll be over to get the letter from you in about an hour. I'm not sure how quickly I can book a flight to St. Lucia, but I'll see what is the cheapest over the next couple days."

"We are covering your expenses. I appreciate frugality, but the next flight would be appreciated. Don't wait just because of cost."

"You're the boss."

"Oh, don't tell Danae that."

We both laughed.

Chapter 5: Money in the Bank

With a letter from James Gilliford, Attorney in Law, in my possession, I called Kelley to discuss the next steps in our investigation. I assumed I would be the one going to the bank in Saint Lucia, but part of being in a partnership is discussing what we were doing and who would be doing what. I explained the situation to her when she answered.

"I'd love to go to Saint Lucia, but I have clients to see here and I think you do better at this part of investigating. Plus, we can't both go. Well, we shouldn't both go. Not on the client's dollar."

"I agree, but I also want this to feel like a true partnership. I know eventually roles will fall into place, but I don't want to assume right now."

"I appreciate that, but I think you need to look at this as you are the president and I'm the vice president. You need to be able to make decisions in this venture without having to stop and consult me and vice versa."

"I'm okay with that. Maybe updates as can. Our version of staff meetings."

"There you go. Again, I appreciate being in this venture with you, but it should not be something that limits us."

With that, I booked a flight down to Saint Lucia. The plane landed in Vieux Fort on the southern portion of the island and I caught a taxi up to Casteries, the capital city in the north and where First National Bank was. Using a bank called First National in Saint Lucia gave me even more reason to believe this escape had been carefully planned by Tony Johnston. The most prevalent bank on the island was the Bank of Saint Lucia, but that would be a give-away if he slipped up and sent something from the bank. There were a lot of First National Banks throughout the world and especially within the United States. The name was simply more generic.

The bank building itself was a modest, two-story building in Casteries. I entered and asked for the accounts manager. After a short time, a middle-aged gentleman came forward.

"Mr. Larson?" He offered his hand and directed me back to his office. "I'm Francois Joseph. How may I be of assistance?"

I complemented Mr. Joseph on the bank and the efficiency that allowed me to see him quickly. "Monsieur Joseph, I believe Mr. Gilliford gave you the basic information. The Kansas Lottery wired money to this bank on behalf of a client but neglected to have proper authorization from all the parties entitled to the funds. This was, of course, the fault of the State of Kansas and your bank bears no fault in receiving these funds. We are merely following up with the individual, Mr. Johnston, so that we can make contact with him to rectify the situation."

Mr. Joseph nodded. "Do you have the letter requested, Mr. Larson?"

I handed Mr. Joseph the letter prepared by James Gilliford. He looked it over and nodded again.

"May I keep this letter for our records?"

"But of course, mon ami." I made a slight bow.

Mr. Joseph smiled and pulled out a small packet. "I am pleased to provide you with these records of the account's activity and the holder's current address."

"Monsieur, I appreciate this. Might there be a small fee for the papers and time."

"The fee for the paperwork is twenty-five dollars, American. I appreciate your understanding of services here."

I handed Mr. Joseph $25 in cash and then provided an additional $50. "For you, mon ami. For your time and cooperation."

"I most graciously accept. Would you care to join me for an afternoon coffee? It is almost time for my break."

"I'd be delighted, Sir."

We walked down the street in Casteries to the Blue Monkey Café. We sat and had some good, strong Caribbean style coffee. I loved it.

"Tell me, Mr. Larson, when do leave our little island?"

"Well, I'd love to stay here. It's beautiful. I have a flight back to the States tomorrow afternoon."

"It is, indeed, unfortunate that you can't spend more time here. Do you have a place to stay?"

“Not yet. I know there are some Sandals resorts and some wonderful hotels. Do you have a recommendation?”

“The Harbour View is not far from here and is both a nice place and inexpensive. I would recommend it for someone staying but a night or two. The all-inclusive resorts are nice, of course, for the visitors who want to be here on the island, but don’t want to necessarily mingle with the locals. You impress me as the type of man who likes experiencing the place he finds himself.”

“Mr. Joseph, I consider that a compliment. Thank you and you are quite correct. And thanks for the recommendation, also. I believe the Harbour View sounds perfect for me.”

“I’m glad to hear it. Let me call and book you a room. When I have clients come in from off the island, I often suggest they stay there.”

Mr. Joseph got on the phone and chatted with the manager at the hotel. He hung up and smiled at me.

“You are booked into one of the nicest rooms overlooking the harbor. I do hope you enjoy your brief stay and will come back.”

"I already consider you as a friend and would be delighted to look you up when I get a chance to return."

"I hope you will, Mr. Larson."

"Please, call me Buck."

"Very well, mon ami. And call me Francois."

We finished our coffees and headed back toward the First National Bank. At the door, we shook hands and Francois gave me directions to the Harbour View from there. I started walking toward the hotel getting stares as I walked with my briefcase. A 6'4" man of Scot-Swedish descent was rather rare on the streets of Casteries.

The directions Francois gave me were perfect and the manager greeted me in person as I came up the steps. He was smiling and talking a mile-a-minute as he escorted me in.

"Francois says you are a man of some importance. I hope you will be satisfied with the room. The water in the shower is not always hot, but it won't be cold either. I sent the maid up just to make sure everything is okay."

"I'm sure it will be just fine. Thank you."

I filled out the register and got my room key. It was an actually key. Not a card. Not a number. A physical key with which to lock and unlock my room.

The room had a balcony overlooking the water and the streets of downtown Casteries. It looked very colonial French in construction and very Caribbean in makeup. The ladies wore colorful dresses and skirts. The streets were narrow and busy. I decided to do a little shopping while here.

I picked up some lightweight pants and a Guayabera style shirt along with some sandals. I found a flowery, colorful sun dress for Kelley and some local style music CDs for both Teddy and Charlie. My travel bag wasn't very big so I had to be judicious while picking up gifts. I enjoyed shopping and spied a couple restaurants that I could try that evening. Just because I was on a work trip didn't mean I couldn't mix in a little fun.

With my purchases back in my room, I changed into the lighter clothing I had just bought. Taking in dinner and maybe check out the local bar scene seemed in order. I looked at the paperwork I had gotten from Francois before heading out. It appeared that Mr. Johnston had settled into Tampico, Mexico. That would also be an interesting trip. One that I was sure I would be taking soon.

I had a nice dinner at a restaurant specializing in local cuisine, and then stopped in at a place called Club Red. The music had a Caribbean sound and there was a small crowd gathering as it approached 10:30 local time. I realized it was just 7:30 back in Eudora which was why I felt a bit more awake. I tried a local drink, the St. Lucia Rum Punch. A couple of guys I met were arguing over whether it should have orange or pineapple juice, so to appease them, I tried both and declared each equally delicious. Both laughed and left it at that. There was no need for an argument.

While the three of us were talking, three ladies came over to our table. One of my new friends was out on the dance floor right away with one of the women whom I assumed he already knew. My other new friend was obviously enamored with the rather buxom young lady beside him. They were riveted on each other, ignoring me and the last girl. The third lady smiled at me and eased into light conversation.

"Where are you from, stranger?" It was an attempt at starting a conversation.

"Is it that obvious that I'm not from here?" I laughed.

She looked around. "Do you see any other white men in here?" She laughed.

"I'm a novelty, I guess."

"A novelty?"

"Unusual. Something not often seen."

"No, the tourist don't usually stop in here. You're funny. What's your name?"

"Buck. What's yours?"

"Zina Charles. I work in a government office downtown."

"Oh. What office?"

"I won't scare you off, if I tell you, will I?"

"I don't know. Sounds ominous. Are you a government spy?"

"I work in police records. It sometimes scares guys."

"Actually, I find that interesting." My comment made her smile. "Would you like to dance?" I stood up as if I knew she would say yes. Or maybe it was to appear confident.

"I'd love to."

I led Zina out to the dance floor, and while I'm not exactly an expert dancer, I felt like I was holding my own. Of course, a couple St. Lucia Rum Punches might have helped. We stayed out on the floor for 4 or 5 dances before coming back to the table. One of my initial acquaintances had already left with his lady friend. The other guy apologized, but said he was leaving, too. He gestured to me as privately as possible toward the girl with him and smiled. I waved him on off. I already gathered I was getting stuck with the bar tab.

"Well, I think I just got stuck with the tab. Would you care for a drink?"

"What were you drinking?"

"I've had two St. Lucia Rum Punches. I will have a third if you'll join me, but that would be about it for me."

"Thank you. I'll have one. It looks like Royalty and Maia have abandoned me to you this evening anyway. You look like a respectable fellow I can trust."

I ordered the drinks and picked up the conversation. "I'm curious, is there a lot of crime here in Casteries?"

"Oh, I imagine it is about the same as anywhere else in the world. Tourists sometimes claim it is more, but I keep records and compare them. It really isn't. I think it's actually less than most major cities in the United States."

"That doesn't surprise me. Americans – I guess technically we are all Americans – those in the U.S. tend to view the rest of the world as more barbaric. Then they wonder why American tourist are seen as the Ugly Americans. People are people. I suspect crime is much worse in New York City than it is here in Casteries. It is a beautiful city here and people are extremely friendly."

"Well, Buck, we have our fair share of swindlers, but the majority of our people are good, honest, hard-working people."

"Tell me about yourself. You seem to like dancing. You work in law enforcement. What else do you like to do?"

"I like reading. Sorry, but I prefer books in French, but I do read English. I like the ocean and go scuba diving when I can. What about you?"

"I love reading, but I can't read much French. I can read Spanish. My favorite thing to relax is to ride motorcycles. I have a 1958 Harley that I ride around at home. I just feel better on a bike."

Zina laughed. "I can picture you riding a big American bike. You don't seem like the café racer type." She looked at my hand for a moment. "Are you married, Buck?"

"No. Was once, but got a divorce. I do have a son. There have been women I've been interested in, but never married again. Admittedly, there is one I very much like, but she is married and therefore off limits to me. Such is my luck in the romance department. Are you married?"

"Give it time, Buck. You do seem like a nice guy. I'm widowed. I married just out of school but my husband died 6 months later in a boating accident. I've never really found anyone else that I am interested in as a husband. I've had offers."

I looked at her athletic frame and beautiful, well-proportioned shape. "I have no doubt about that."

"It's hard being alone, though. In some ways, I feel angry at him, like I've been abandoned here. It's not rational, but it is the way you feel."

"But that's understandable. It doesn't have to be rational as a feeling. It's better to recognize the feeling and know it's not rational. A much healthier way of dealing with it."

We talked about our lives and shared our thoughts, and fell into an ease in chatting. She finally looked at her watch.

"Oh my! I need to get home. I still work tomorrow. Where are you staying?"

"I have a room for the night at the Harbour View. I fly back tomorrow."

"I live just beyond the hotel. Would you mind walking with me home? I'd rather not have to get a cab and walking alone isn't smart at this time of night."

"I would be delighted." I paid the tab which wasn't as much as I was afraid it might be, fortunately having some East Caribbean currency, and we left. She slid her arm into the crook of my elbow. It was comfortable out as we walked along the streets under a clear, starry sky.

Zina looked at the stars while she sang a little song as we walked. It was a sweet little melody, but she said she didn't know the name of it. It was just something she heard as a child. We were at her house well before I wanted to arrive. The night was cooling but still quite comfortable.

"I hope you'll come back sometime. It would be nice to see you again."

"Thank you. I'd enjoy seeing you again, too. You've certainly made this an enjoyable evening for me." I exchanged numbers with her telling her to call me if she got to the States. We kissed and hugged and then I made sure she got inside her house okay before turning back toward the hotel.

Sometimes you just meet people for an evening that you connect well with. There isn't any more to it. Just a person who makes your life and living it better for that brief moment. I strolled easily back to my hotel. This business trip had become the relaxation I needed in my life. It was funny that I was getting paid for doing it.

I slept a peaceful night and was driven back to St. Lucia's International Airport in plenty of time for my return flight to Kansas City via Atlanta. Before I got on the plane, I wondered what Zina would be doing. Just a person who popped up in my life and likely wouldn't see again. There are so many people in our lives that this is the truth. I wondered if she would be wondering what I was doing this morning. We had just been the proverbial two ships that pass in the night.

The flight back was uneventful. I had a brief lay-over in Atlanta but not really enough to make an update call to Kelley. It would have to wait until I was back in Kansas City. I texted Ed to see if he could pick me up at the airport when I arrived. He texted back that he wasn't a taxi service and asked what time he should be there. It's good to have friends like Ed.

He was waiting when I got off the plane. He was in his police uniform which meant everyone basically left him alone. I had traveled light, so we didn't have to go to the baggage claim area.

"Eudora still safe with you out of town?" I asked as I handed him the small box of Cuban cigars I had picked up for him in Saint Lucia.

"Safer. Thanks for the illegal smokes. How was your latest junket?"

"Picked up the info I needed." I paused. "And I had a good time. Went out dancing."

"Dancing! What a useless activity."

"Your wife doesn't think so. She enjoys it when you get her out on the dance floor."

"Probably because I don't do it that often. You ever think of that? Don't give her any ideas." We laughed. "What's your next step, Buck?"

"I need to call my partner and update her. Then I need to call my client. After that, I suspect I'll be biking down to old Mexico."

"Mexico?! What the hell for? And why bike down?"

"The missing guy appears to be in Tampico and because I love biking."

"You, my friend, are crazy."

"That I am."

Once home, I gave Kelley a call to update her on the case.

"So they just gave you the address? I'm surprised."

"Things work differently down there. Sometimes a little easier. It's a friendly place."

"Friendly? Did you make some friends?"

"Of course. The accounts manager went with me for coffee and pointed out a nice hotel to stay at for the evening. Then I ran into some nice locals at a club and got to dance with a very pretty lady."

"I see. Can't leave you alone for a second without the girls finding you!" Kelley laughed.

"Good people all over the world."

"How good?"

"Walked her home. Said goodnight and then went to my hotel room. She works in the city police office."

"Well, of course it's none of my business except you know I worry. You do have a thing, though, for the law enforcement types."

"I know. I worry, too. I understand. You're jealous."

She was quiet for a moment and must have decided to let the last comment slide. "So, what's next?"

"I need to call Gilliford and let him know what's going on. I suspect the next step is going to Mexico to confront Johnston."

"Do you need me to go down there with you?"

"Do you want to go? I was planning on taking the Harley, but if you want to go, too, I can change up to a rental car."

"The Harley! Are you crazy?!"

"Hmmm, I'm getting that asked a lot lately. No, it's as good as any other ride. Actually, better."

"Buck, it's Mexico! Bandidos! Drug gangs!"

"Whoa! That myth ought to stop. There is danger there, but no more than in New York, Chicago, or even Kansas City. We tend to dismiss our drug and gang violence as isolated and ramp it up when it's the rest of the world. You just have to be smart about things, just like you have to be smart about things here."

"You're right. But I worry. I don't think I'll be any help in Mexico and it would just be an added expense."

"We could go dancing. Protect me from all the women that you say I draw to me. Besides, I picked you up a pretty sun dress that I would love to see you in."

"You! I worry more about you wanting to see me without any dress, but thank you. I'm sure you will be fine. I just want to do my part."

"Kelley, you provide a different skill set. Not that you couldn't do the leg work, but that's a waste of your talents. You're the thinker. I'm the one who works in the trenches. It's the way we work as a team."

"Okay. If they do want you to go down there to confront him, what can you do?"

"Actually, not much. He hasn't really committed a crime. I can't make him come back. I guess it would be just letting him know that he can be found, and his money could be tied up."

"Does someone need to go down there to do that?"

"In person has impact. The question is do they send me, the investigator, or maybe take his wife down there. That might be too much for him or for her. I guess we will see what the client wants us to do."

"I'm still surprised they gave you so much information at the bank."

I called James Gilliford's office and spoke with the ever-efficient Ms. Oldson. She told me she would have Mr. Gilliford call me as soon as he was available. I realized that she meant that she would have him call when she felt he was available to make the call. Ironically, Mr. Gilliford called me for an update obviously not getting the message from his secretary.

"Buck, I hadn't heard from you since you went down to St. Lucia. How'd it go?"

I decided that it was best to avoid mentioning I had called and left a message at his office. I'm sure Ms. Oldson had a note on her pad ready to give Mr. Gilliford at some time. "Very successful. I have an address. In fact, I was wondering how you wanted me to proceed? Do you want me to go down to Tampico, Mexico to confront him?"

"Hmmm, that's a good question. Technically, you've found him, but it would be good to have confirmation. What would you do if you confront him?"

"Not much I can do. Not a crime so far. I've been thinking about options. Your client could go down and confront him. If she needed, I could go along."

"I wouldn't recommend it to her, but she might want to do that. Not sure what that would do? She's received my update regarding the found account and your work up through now. I guess he wouldn't even have to answer the door. And what if he's moved on?"

"You can send him a letter at that address with whatever information or demands you think appropriate."

"I've already drafted a hold on his account in St. Lucia and had his wife sign the letter. It might be best if someone actually verified he is at the address in Mexico, though."

"I can go down and either just verify he is there or confront him about his leaving if he is there."

"I think verifying he's there is all we should ask of you. If you can observe or pick up any other information - without letting on you're a private investigator - that might help."

"Okay. I'll head down tomorrow. I should have the Harley ready to roll."

"You're taking the Harley down there!"

"Yep! No need to fly and then rent a car."

"Good luck! I guess you know what you're doing."

I called Kelley back and let her know the plan. She still thought I was a little crazy for wanting to ride the Harley down there. But she knew she couldn't talk me out of it. Tomorrow, I would be headed south to Mexico to say 'Hola' to Senior Johnston or at least make sure he was still there.

Chapter 6: South of the Border

I looked at the address again as I prepared my saddle bags for the trip south of the border. The house was on Calle Loma Nortena in Tampico. I laughed. There was a Walmart not far from the house according to my internet search. The American wasn't going totally Mexican while down Mexico way.

The Harley was packed and I got an early start, heading out as the sun was coming up. Riding south out of Eudora I headed down to Ottawa and caught I-35 south toward Emporia. I usually don't like the interstate routes, but the trip to Mexico was already going to be a two-day adventure down. I refueled on the far side of Wichita and got back on I-35 near the casino there. The sun was growing higher and it was moving from a comfortable ride to getting hot. I was staring to sweat. The air baking me as I cut through it.

For a break, I decided to grab lunch in Oklahoma City. There was a Cracker Barrel so I knew I could grab breakfast for lunch, a favorite thing for me while traveling. I discovered that I was actually in Edmond, a suburb of Oklahoma City. As long as I could get one of the breakfast samplers, it didn't matter to me. Filling up on food in this heat could be a problem so I paced myself and had plenty of water.

Since I had stopped for lunch, I refueled again even though I really didn't need to. I just figured it helped extend the ride time and reduce the down time. Part of the reason I didn't like interstate on the bike is it pushed the concept of destination instead of the ride, but this was one time when destination was absolutely the point. I was going to Tampico.

After clearing Oklahoma and rolling into Texas, I knew I'd be in for a mess around Dallas. Metropolitan sprawl around Dallas and Houston created backed up traffic that rivaled, at times, the traffic jams around Los Angeles and New York City. It was also helpful I didn't need to fuel up in the Dallas-Fort Worth area and could keep on going. I pushed on to Waco to fill up and then pushed past Austin, stopping for the night in San Antonio, a beautiful little city.

I managed to get a room at the Hotel Indigo near the Riverwalk. The front desk clerk gave me a disdainful look as I walked in, but let me know a safe place to garage my bike as well as giving me a room overlooking the Riverwalk. I lay down on the bed for just a bit in my room before giving Kelley a call.

"The Riverwalk? In San Antonio?" Kelley sounded impressed.

"Yes, you'd love it. It's bright and friendly. Wish you were here."

"You made good time. I've wanted to go. Now I am jealous."

"You should come down on vacation here. It's scenic, not that I'll see much. I'll be in Tampico tomorrow. Anything new?"

"No. I still wonder about the bank giving you that address so easily. Be careful."

I assured her I would as I hung up the phone. It was time to stretch my legs and grab a late supper. The pathway along the Riverwalk was lined with restaurants and bars. A passenger barge passed by followed by a dining barge with people enjoying a meal while out on the river. The atmosphere was lively, but the pace was relaxed. I came upon the Hard Rock Café as I walked. As much as I had heard about the restaurant chain, I had never eaten at one so it was time to try.

It had the regular fare of many upscale chain restaurants. I wasn't disappointed in the food, but I reminded myself that eating local made these travels better. I decided that riding interstate had "dumbed down" my mind. I was acting like a typical tourist. A further indicator to avoid interstates and stay to the blue highways whenever I could.

It had been a long day of riding and once back in my room, I was asleep as soon as my head hit the pillow. I dreamed of being in the old West, riding with the Texas Rangers, and moving from town-to-town chasing outlaws. Had we really come very far from the 1880s? Sometimes it didn't seem like it.

I was up early and checked out of my room. I looked at the maps. I-35 would take me to Laredo which would require me to cut back to the coast at some point. I decided on I-37 toward Corpus Christi. I could cut south on U.S. 281 and cross the border at Reynosa, taking Highway 97 on south when in Mexico. I filled up with gas and bought some fuel booster before crossing over. The octane level in Mexico sometimes wasn't as high as U.S. gas and the Harley would need the boost. The crossing itself was easy, I had my passport card, although the Mexican border agents were very interested in the old Harley. I don't blame them. It is an usual bike - very old school.

I chatted with the Mexican border agents for a short bit and they gave me a little insight about where to ride and where to avoid in route to Tampico. It was much appreciated. I bid them an adieu, then took 97 south to Highway 101 and then cut south again on Highway 180. Daytime travel was fine. and I didn't have any trouble getting into Tampico. It was getting well into the afternoon or early evening, but I finally found the address on Calle Loma Nortena. I pulled up so I could watch the house for a bit. It was a nice place but not overly ostentatious. I'm sure it had cost Mr. Johnston a pretty penny.

A city police car rolled by and stopped. The officer got out and tapped me on the shoulder.

"Que esta hiciendo, Senor?"

"Soy un detective y cree que se encuentra en este casa un hombre que desaparece en los Estados Unidos."

"You think a man missing from the U.S. lives there?"

"Yes. I just want to be sure."

"Vamanos! Vamos a ver." The officer signaled for me to follow him up to the house. Subtlety was not in the cards for this case. It wasn't the way I planned to check on him, but this might work.

The officer knocked on the door and we waited. There was movement inside. A lady opened the door. She was in her late 30s or early 40s, still attractive. She wore a yellow dress with red trim.

"Si?"

"Esta aqui un Senor …?" The office looked at me to give him the name.

"Johnston."

The lady looked at me but nodded. "Si. El vive aqui."

The officer continued, tipping his hat. "Podemos hablar con Sr., umm Johnston?"

We were shown into the house and directed to some chairs in the living room. The woman left us calling out for Antonio. A moment later Tony Johnston stepped into the room. He looked at the officer and then me.

"Senor, this gentleman says he is looking for you. That you went missing from the United States. Is that true?" The officer showed no signs of joking around. He made sure Johnston saw his badge and the full uniform of a Tampico Police Officer including his Sam Browne gear with pistol.

"Sort of. Am I in some sort of trouble here?"

The officer shook his head and looked at me. "Is he, Senor?"

I shook my head. "Not criminal trouble really."

"Okay." The officer started to leave and then turned around looking at me. "And what is your name, Senor?"

"Buck. Buck Larson." I reached out to shake the officer's hand. He took it and then bowed.

"I will be passing back by here in a bit. I don't want anything to happen to that nice motorcycle of yours."

Tony Johnston looked at me. "You came down here on a motorcycle?"

"A Harley. A '58 Duo-Glide actually." The officer stepped out. "You kind of ran out on a wife and pregnant girlfriend."

"I know. I had to. It was too much."

The lady who had answered the door came into the room. Both Tony and I stood up.

"This is Esmerelda Hernandez." Ms. Hernandez curtsied. "We live together here. I don't think my family would understand, but Esme is the woman for me. They are more worried about appearances."

"Look, Tony. I've been simply hired to find you. We know you hit the lottery which allowed you to slip out without much of a trail at first, but my partner and I found it. You can't just simply disappear. Not in this day and age."

"I know I'm being a heel, but I felt forced into marrying Carla. It was a family thing. I don't think she loves me either. Aimee was a fling. She was an escape from Carla. Not that Carla was a bad woman. I never wanted a child with Carla or Aimee. I never intended to leave Carla for Aimee or anyone else. I think I hoped Carla would discover my infidelity and file for a divorce on her own. And now I've hit the lottery and found Esmerelda. I just want to be with her. I'd like to have a family with her."

I looked around. Esmerelda had left the room quietly.

"Well, technically, you're still married. Why not take care of that situation first and make things right. I don't know what to tell you about Aimee. Seems to be no doubt the child is yours according to her."

"Yes, it's mine."

"Well, and according to Kansas law, half the lottery money belongs to Carla. It doesn't matter that you tried to hide it outside the United States."

"Let me talk with Esmerelda first. Then I will make arrangements to rectify everything. I should have just taken care of things at first. I've know that the day would come when eventually I was discovered. I just didn't think it would be so soon."

I nodded and headed out to my bike. The officer was parked behind it, sipping a cup of coffee as he watched me approach. He was definitely keeping an eye on the situation for me. He got out as I walked up.

"So, Senor Larson, is everything going to be okay?"

"Well, Antonio might not think so, but he says he's going to do the right thing. That means divorcing his wife and sharing some of the money he won;

and hopefully, taking care of a child that is on the way."

"Some men just have to be guided into doing the right thing. I don't think he will back out of doing the moral thing now." He paused. "Tell me about your bike, amigo. It's a beauty."

"Thanks. I got it from an old farmer I used to work for. I fixed it up a bit and put a new engine in it. The saddle bags are from a leather shop up in Indiana."

"I wish my wife would let me get a motorcycle. It would be fun. But we have 5 kids. Three sons and two daughters."

"A big family, my friend."

"My pride and joy. My eldest boy wants to be a police officer like me. I want him to become a lawyer. My youngest boy wants to be a professional soccer player. Ah, the dreams of youth. The middle one wants to study history at the university and both girls want to become nurses."

We both saw Tony Johnston come running out of the house. He was yelling.

"I have to get back to the States! I have to!"

"Calmate, Senor. Por que tan rapido?"

"My money is gone! All of it!"

I looked at him. "What do you mean your money is gone?"

"The account in Saint Lucia has been wiped clean. I hadn't set up an account here yet. I tried to book a flight back and my payment was rejected. When I checked the bank balance, it's basically zero. They said a Mrs. Johnston signed for it. Took it in the form of a cashier's check."

I was glad I had included Mexico and Canada on my phone plan. It still wasn't cheap to call, but cheaper than trying to make a call without the plan. I called James Gilliford's office. Ms. Oldson answered.

"I'll be happy to give him the message, Mr. Larson, as …"

"Now you listen to me and you listen good. I'm not playing games with you this time. Put me in contact with Mr. Gilliford RIGHT NOW! Do you understand?!"

"There is no need to be huffy, Mr. Larson."

"The hell there isn't. Now, damn it!"

There was a pause and then finally Gilliford picked up.

"Buck? What's up? Ms. Oldson is throwing fits."

"I've got Johnston. Apparently though, all the money from the Saint Lucia account he set up is gone."

"Well, that explains it."

"Explains what?"

"I have just received envelopes from Mrs. Johnston that she asked me to open when you actually found Tony. The first one is to me." I could hear the envelope being ripped open and then a laugh. "I'll read it to you, Buck. It says, Mr. Gilliford, thank you for your help. Here is a cashier's check for your services which I believe more than covers your fees. And, yes, Buck, it more than covers my fees. She says she has also provided an envelope that I am to give to the Morelli and Larson Detective Agency which contains more than sufficient payment for your services. She also included an envelope to be given to Mr. Anthony Johnston upon his return. It includes terms for divorce which he may take. Included is a Power of Attorney for me,

Mr. Gilliford to act on my best interest in a divorce proceeding. I never wish to see Tony again." I could hear him take a deep breath. "Shall I open your envelope?"

"You might as well."

"There is a cashier's check to your detective agency and a letter. It reads, Mr. Larson and Dr. Morgan, Thank you for your service and work. I hope you don't feel duped or cheated by this, but upon finding that Tony not only had a girlfriend which he impregnated, I find he hit the lottery and ran off without even a word, I am taking the funds from the account you found and holding onto the money. If it makes you feel better know that I will give Tony a portion once he has agreed to the divorce terms I've provided to Mr. Gilliford. Unlike him, I don't want to deny him a portion, but it will be under my terms. I may appear a bit of wilting flower, but my strength is in my grounding. Again, thank you both for all you did for me."

"Wow!"

"Exactly!"

Tony tapped me on the shoulder. "So what's up?"

"Basically, you messed with the wrong woman, buddy."

"What do you mean?"

"You need to find a way back to Kansas and take care of your mess before you get any money. Or stay here and start all over from scratch."

"She took it?"

"She took it all. But, in a way, you're lucky. She says she is willing to return a portion if you do things her way. She wants that divorce you should have asked for in the first place."

Tony walked back to the house there on Calle Loma Nortena. A suitcase sat on the front porch. He looked up. Esmerelda was looking at him from behind the front door.

"Take care of what you should have done. Maybe when you do that, well, maybe I might see you. Now go." She turned away from the door leaving him there.

The officer laughed. "Amigo, you better start walking. You have a long way to go and no means to get there other than your feet."

Tony looked at me. "Can I hitch a ride back to Kansas?"

"Sure. But not on my bike. I don't mean to be cruel, but I'm not hauling you on my Harley. I won't put my bike through that."

The officer and I laughed. I suppose it isn't proper, but it just seemed just. The tables had clearly turned on Anthony Johnston.

I started up my bike for the return trip. The officer waved.

"Vaya con Dios! Come visit sometime, Sr. Buck!"

"Take care, my friend. Bring your family up to Kansas sometime for a visit. I have plenty of space."

I headed north. I saw Tony get into the back of the police cruiser. I guessed he was going to at least get a ride to the bus station if he was lucky. Or maybe going to jail as a vagrant if the officer wanted to push the point. I'd wait until getting to the border to give Kelley the good news. The case was solved.

On the Rocks

Chapter 7: Until Death Do Us Part

Kelley was out at the house as we celebrated wrapping up our first case as the Morelli and Larson Detective Agency. It was the first time Victor had come to the house. Kelley had said that he was doing well with his problem and had agreed to do more social gatherings with her. If Kelley was happy, then I was happy for her. Patrick, their son, was relaxing on the deck, playing a video game on a tablet while his sister, Charlie and my son, Teddy enjoyed a little food and talked about where they wanted to go to college. Kelley and I had resigned ourselves to the idea that our kids would be heading off, at least at first, to the same college, and that this had all the appearances of a long-term relationship. Even more of a reason Victor should start coming to get-togethers here at the house.

Tina, our administrative assistant, was in attendance with a new boyfriend. Danny Dunwiddy seemed perfect for Tina. He was attentive and kind to her. They laughed and giggled while hanging together in a corner, out of the way. Both are rather shy but together they come out of their shells.

Ed and Erin Hatfield were there. It just wouldn't feel right to celebrate without them. Ed and I went way back and he was currently Chief of Police for the little berg of Eudora. We had both served in the National Guard in the same unit. He kept talking about retirement, but we all knew he never really would.

Dr. Danae Cornwall, Kelley's psychology partner and Danae's boyfriend, James Gilliford were the other guests. Gilliford was the attorney who gave us our first case. He still seemed a bit awkward as even he was surprised about the client's actions. I was pleased to have had a case and we had been paid handsomely.

Ed laughed about the results. "Man, Buck, that guy sure got what he deserved. I heard he made it back to the States okay."

James Gilliford nodded. "He is more than willing to agree to the terms of the divorce. He's hoping he can get some money out of this. The girlfriend he got pregnant is demanding support. His family is trying to take care of the medical expenses so that there is a healthy birth. I think they want the mother to let the grandparents raise the child."

Kelley pulled me aside. "Do you think Mr. Johnston will be okay? I know he was a real ass, but people tend to overdo the guilt with these situations. Deserved or not, it doesn't help."

"I think he is going to try and salvage what he can financially here; then head back to Mexico to see if he can win back Esmerelda. I think she might take him back, but she's a smart girl. She will want him to take care of everything here first so that she doesn't have to deal with it, too."

"I'd like to meet her some day. She sounds … well, strong."

Charlie and Teddy came up to us dragging Victor over with them. They were smiling and giddy. It made me worry what they might say.

"Dad," Teddy began, "we were wondering if we - you, me, Charlie and her family - could make a college visit to Chapel Hill before the summer is over?"

I was relieved. I almost expected an announcement that they had decided to get married already. "I'm certainly up for it and your mom's family is out in Wilmington for a bit, so she could come up. UNC is an excellent school."

Kelley looked at me with a bit of a worried look. Victor spoke up instead. "That sounds wonderful. It would be helpful and be a good vacation." Kelley turned to Victor and smiled.

"Sounds like we can plan something. You and Charlie need to find out from the school when it is feasible to make a visit. I suspect Charlie will want to talk to the girls' basketball coach."

My phone rang. It was Jackie McFadden from Mt. Vernon, Indiana. She was an attorney for the foundation I ran there, the Dawn Stevens Memorial Foundation.

"Hello, Jackie. How are you doing?"

"I'm fine. I hope I'm not bothering you right now."

"No problem. We're just celebrating the detective agency's successful conclusion of our first case."

"Congrats. That's kind of what I'd like to talk to you about. I would like to hire your agency personally to look into a matter."

"Sounds serious. What's up?"

“I have, well had a friend who died recently. It was ruled accidental poisoning, but I think there is more to it. I’d like you to look into it.”

I motioned Kelley to listen with me. “Go on. Why do you think it’s more than accidental poisoning?”

“First of all, Vicky Ann had some concerns about her husband, Kevin. She thought he was up to something illegal or underhanded, but she didn’t know what.”

“Do you know why she thought that?”

“Not really. We were going to get together at my office, but she died from poisoning before she made it over.”

“What was she poisoned with?”

“Cyanide. They said there were wild cherry and peach pits on her side table where she had been drinking. They think she bit the pits so hard that they cracked open and the cyanide leaked into her system.”

“Cyanide is one of the most toxic poisons but also has a very bitter taste. You would think she’d notice the odd flavor.”

"She was drinking Gin and Tonic. They said the quinine in the tonic probably masked the taste."

"Did the police check the gin and the tonic for traces of the poison?"

"Yes. Nothing in either, but there was in her glass. They suggested she tried to spit out the poison into the glass when she finally realized she had it in her system. Can you look into it for me? I just don't think it happened how the police say it did."

I looked at Kelley. She shrugged. "It seems like something we can do, Buck."

"We will look into it. I'll be in town there tomorrow."

Kelley tapped me on the shoulder. "We will be in town."

"Correction, Jackie. WE will be in town tomorrow to look into it."

"Thanks, Buck."

I hung up and when Kelley and I turned around, the whole party was staring at us.

"Well, friends, this is not only a celebration of completing our first case, but the assignment of our second."

The group let out a cheer and the party continued. I walked over to Victor.

"Are you okay with Kelley coming on the case with me?"

"Kelley is going to do what she thinks she ought to do. She's partnered with you, so she is going to want to do her part. It makes me a little nervous. I know you have strong feelings for Kelley, but I also know you have a strong moral base when it comes to marriage and relationships and Kelley does, too. Besides, it will give me some time to bond with the kids." He started to turn away. "Oh, but please don't take too long to solve this."

I laughed and Kelley came back over.

"What was that about?"

"Making sure your husband is okay with you coming on this case."

"He knows I'd go anyway. But what if it did bother him?"

"Then I'd know it was bothering him."

"Buck, what am I going to do with you?"

"I really don't know, but since you're coming along, I'm guessing the Harley will have to rest. My Jeep or your Jaguar?" I saw the look on her face. "The Jag it is. Pick me up about 7:00?"

"Why so late?" She laughed.

I had a thermos of coffee ready and my travel bag packed before Kelley arrived. It was 6:45. The sun was already shining. I knew she'd be early. She seemed surprised that everything was by the door waiting to go.

"There's no catching you by surprise."

"I try to avoid it. At least we will be hitting Kansas City before the rush really hits."

"I don't mind. Kansas City isn't as bad as most major cities."

Kelley was right. It was rare that traffic fully backed up around the Kansas City area. If it did, it was due to construction or a ballgame out at the stadium complex or a wreck. Even negotiating downtown wasn't too bad.

Jackie had sent me a copy of the police report so I could review it. I pulled it out to go over with Kelley as she drove.

"It looks like they did a cursory examination in the case. Lab results show no cyanide in the Gin bottle or in the Tonic water. Cyanide in the glass she was drinking from. Peach pits and wild cherry pits on the table with some of them cracked."

"Aren't those pits extremely hard to crack?"

"I think so, but I suppose if you gnaw or grind on them it could open up. Or if one is bad and gone soft. Maybe someone thinking about something long and hard or who had a nervous habit that led to biting down."

"But if you cracked open one, you'd think you'd know it."

"True, unless you were so preoccupied with something or it had been a habit for a while. Stomach contents show cyanide, gin, tonic, cucumbers - apparently she ate cucumber sandwiches - bread, lettuce and even little bits of fingernail. She must have been one of those nervous ones who chew on her fingernails which would fit when worried."

"Where was the husband?"

I looked through the report. "Kevin Hayes had left shortly after getting home from work to hang out with some friends at his club. He was there with tons of witnesses from before supper until around 11:30 when he got back home, found his wife keeled over and called 9-1-1."

"Pretty tight alibi."

"I don't think they were looking for much with the other evidence. The police have no reason to doubt him."

I scanned through the rest of the report. It was pretty straight forward. The assessment was accidental death due to the unintended ingestion of poison.

"So where do we start when we get there?"

"I imagine we talk to Jackie and get more on why she thinks the death wasn't accidental and go from there. She seems to think the husband committed some foul play, but I don't see it here in this report."

I suggested staying at the Tropicana in Evansville. It's a nice hotel overlooking the Ohio River and it would give us a nice base to work out of for our investigation. We were given 2 adjoining rooms on the uppermost floor.

"I see there is a casino attached to the hotel."

"Hotels with casinos generally have nicer accommodations for a better price. They hope to get you to play longer and stay longer." I knew Victor had a gambling issue. "Are you okay staying here? Victor is the gambler, not you."

"Oh, it's fine. I just won't mention the casino when I talk to him. It will feel like rubbing his nose in his issue. These rooms and the view are very nice."

"Let's rest a moment and then head over to Mount Vernon to talk to Jackie."

We both just threw our bags aside in our rooms. I've rarely used dressers in hotel rooms. I walked over and knocked on Kelley's door.

"Ready!" she called out. She opened her door. "These are really nice rooms."

We walked back to her car in the hotel's garage.

"So, is Jackie married?"

I smiled at Kelley. "No. She does have a daughter about Charlie's age. She's quite the volleyball player. You ought to talk to Jackie about her searches for colleges with Beth."

"I will. I was just curious. She helps with the foundation you head up."

"Yes. She was the attorney for the Stevens family so it made sense."

We headed west out of Evansville and were in Mount Vernon about 15 minutes later. Kelley pulled up to Jackie's office. Getting out of the car, I caught Kelley taking a quick assessment of how she looked out of the corner of my eye before going in. I laughed quietly.

Inside the law office, we were taken almost immediately into Jackie's interior office. She had papers neatly stacked in various places on her desk. She pulled one stack toward her to refer to.

"Good to see you, Buck. Are you two staying at your house here in Mount Vernon?"

Kelley looked questioningly at me.

"Well, I want to be able to work with my partner and I didn't think it would be appropriate right now to stay at Dawn's old house." I probably should have asked Kelley if she would have preferred staying at the house in Mount Vernon, but it did feel awkward and I had avoided it.

"That makes sense. And the incident I want you to look into happened over in Evansville."

Kelley stuck out her hand. "By the way, since Buck hasn't introduced us yet, I'm his partner Kelley Morgan."

Jackie took her hand smiling. "Well, he is a guy." Guy was not used as a compliment, but the ladies were bonding some.

I cleared my throat for attention. "Jackie, why do you think this is more than an accident?"

She looked at some papers on her desk. "I wrote down some remembrances, but these were not written down at the time." I nodded. It was a lawyer's caveat to having notes that can't be legally used. "Vicky had told me a couple months or so ago that Kevin had started acting funny. That he seemed nervous and agitated about work and more distant at home."

"What kind of work does Mr." Kelley paused realizing she didn't have their last name in front of her.

"Hayes," I interjected.

"Hayes. What kind of work does he do?"

"He owns - well, co-owns - a small manufacturing company."

"Who is the co-owner? I assume his wife." I was curious if there was an outside owner.

"Well, yes, his wife owned a third as did he. There was a third investor by the name of Stanford Ellington. He was a silent partner in the true sense. He didn't make any decisions about the business operations; just made his investment and shared in profits."

"So now Mr. Hayes has a two-thirds share making him the sole decision maker," Kelley observed.

"Exactly."

Kelley pushed on. "How is the company doing?"

"Squeaking by. The market for the gadgets they make seems to be dwindling. Vicky told me several times that she didn't think they were making the changes needed to keep up to the changing demand."

"Did she say why?" I asked.

"Kevin likes to rest on laurels and doesn't do well with changes. It was once a top manufacturer, but no longer. He's kind of lazy."

"Why didn't Vicky push for the changes?" Kelley added, "I sure would have."

"She wasn't as interested in the company and she didn't want to make Kevin feel demeaned. I think she would have been okay just being a small manufacturing company."

"Jackie," I asked, "what else makes you think it was foul play?"

"More recently, Vicky said she was really concerned about Kevin. That he seemed to be losing it and she told me she was scared for him and herself."

"But the police thought it was just an accident. I saw the report you sent me. Did she usually drink gin and tonic?"

"That was her 'coper.' The drink that helped her cope with stress and unwind. She generally had one or two every evening lately."

"What about peaches and wild cherries?"

"She liked fresh fruit. I don't recall her eating that specific combination, but she liked apples, pears, peaches, cherries, wild berries, melon. She'd rather have that than any meat and she wasn't much of a salad person, but she picked up a taste for cucumber sandwiches."

Kelley nodded. "What about insurance? Do you know if there was life insurance on her?"

Jackie smiled. "There was. I contacted the insurance company and let them know I was considering private investigation. They indicated that they would be willing to cover costs if it turned out not to be an accident and are withholding payment pending your investigation."

"Does Kevin know that?" I asked.

"I don't think he knows that I started it. The insurance agent is going to tell him that the money is being withheld pending the outcome of an independent investigation."

"I wonder what his reaction to that will be." I paused. "Can I get a copy of your recollections? I realize those can't be used as direct evidence since you wrote them down well after the events, but they might be helpful to us as we look at the case."

"Sure. I'll make you a copy." Jackie got up to make a copy. "Buck, thanks for doing this."

"No problem. By the way, how's Beth doing?"

"She's great. Looks like she's going to I.U. for college. Pre-Law on a volleyball scholarship."

"Congratulations. Not too far from home, but a little independence up in Bloomington."

"Scares me a little."

"My daughter is being recruited by some colleges," Kelley noted. "Any tips, hints or warnings for me?"

"Is she a volleyball player?"

"Well, she's being recruited for basketball."

"My advice is to listen to see if they talk about the academic programs your daughter would be interested in first. Let's face it, not many are going pro in sports; and for women, it's even tougher than men."

Kelley nodded. "Thanks."

We headed out of Jackie's office and back to her car. She stopped before getting in.

"Can I see this house you have here? Or will that be too painful? I admit that I'm curious."

"Sure. Let's go by. It's just down the street on Main."

We drove by and I had Kelley park out back by the garage. She noted the old carriage house.

"It's a neat, old building. An old carriage house. Do you know how old it is?"

"It was built in the 1870s, I've been told."

We walked up to the house and I unlocked the door. Memories flooded in. Everything was as I left it. I walked into the kitchen and asked Kelley if she wanted a coffee. She came into the kitchen.

"I'd love a cup."

I popped a K-cup into the coffee maker and got her cup brewing first. "My guess is Jackie put creamer in the fridge."

Kelley opened the refrigerator and there was a small bottle of Italian

Sweet Cream. "Does Jackie always fix you up here?"

"I generally stay here when I do work for the Foundation so she's been helpful in keeping some basics restocked."

"That's nice. Why aren't you two dating?"

"Oh, she was good friends with Dawn. She is the attorney for the Foundation I head up. I'm more interested in someone else."

Kelley blushed. "Still, she seems smart and she's pretty."

"So is the lady I'm interested in."

"But she's married."

"Maybe I like that she's unreachable. You're the psychologist. You might know."

"I just might. Do you mind showing me around the house? It is a really neat Victorian."

I gave her the tour. Looking at the furnishings, I wondered if I ought to replace them. The furniture kind of fit the house though. I still struggled with giving it up, yet also with keeping it when it was used so little.

We went upstairs to the master bedroom. An armoire was against the near wall. The old brass bed was there, centered against the far wall.

"That's a cool old bed."

I smiled. "It is different. I like it."

Kelley jumped up on the bed and then went ahead and sprawled across it. "It's comfy."

I watched her lying there. She looked at me and then got up. I laughed.

"I'm sorry," Kelley offered. "I guess I was unintentionally pushing it."

"You're okay. But yes, seeing you on my bed is tough."

"Let's go back downstairs. We need to refocus on the case."

We went down and had our coffee. "I'll get ahold of the Evansville Police and see about getting an appointment to see their files and talk to them." I picked up my phone and dialed. After a couple reconnections, I was able to get an appointment made.

"Looks like we are in to see them tomorrow morning."

Kelley finished her coffee. I cleaned our cups and I locked up as we were leaving.

"Are you sure you don't want to stay here?"

"I think we are better off staying there in Evansville."

"Safer?"

"Yes, safer for you. Safer for me in one regard."

"Oh, what's that?"

"Kelley, you know how I feel. And you know I want to do the right thing by you. Just avoiding temptation."

"Aw, that's sweet. You find me a temptress."

"Kelley! That's not what I said."

She laughed and we headed back to Evansville.

We got back to our rooms. I knew I just wanted to relax a moment. I had kicked off my boots and laid back. There was a knock.

"Come on in," I called out.

Kelley walked in. Seeing me on the bed she sat in a chair across from it to chat. "What do you think we should do for supper? I'm getting a little hungry and I don't want to eat in or around the casino."

"Well, how about pizza and beer?"

"Now that sounds good. Know of a place?"

"Turoni's Pizzery and Brewery. It's good and I love the name. It's not far."

"So, are you going to get up?"

"Gee, Mom! I don't want to get up yet."

Kelley laughed and jumped on top of me. The bed squeaked.

"Come on! Let's grab a bite."

I rolled her over so I was on top. Then I bared my teeth. She giggled. I took a breath and got up.

"Alright. Let's go grab something."

"For a minute, I thought you were grabbing something."

I tossed a pillow at her. "Stop playing. I may not be able to stop sometime."

"I sometimes wonder if that would be so bad." I took a step toward Kelley and she backed up. "Okay! Okay!"

I got my boots back on. She fixed her hair and looked at me. "Buck, I am glad I can be playful with you. Sometimes I need things to be light. Thanks."

I smiled. Walking over, I grabbed her and gave her a big hug and she hugged me back. I let go. "Come on, partner."

We made it over to Turoni's and found a table. We both had a Peroni and ordered a mushroom and Italian sausage pizza to share. There were several people, a lot of them families there in the restaurant.

"Buck, I'm not sure why, but I agree with Jackie. I think there is something more than an accident there."

"Well, I trust you and I trust Jackie, but proving it is not as easy. I'd say you just had woman's intuition, but I suspect there is something just not adding up and you're both sensing it. It just isn't coming to light yet."

Our pizza came out and we dropped talking about the case for a bit. Our own kids were a better topic anyway.

"You know, I won't be surprised if Teddy and Charlie end up engaged after they get to college."

"I've thought about that. Wouldn't surprise me either. They seem pretty well set on each other. And they seem to be level-headed about the relationship."

"I agree. I talked to Charlie about sex. After the awkward start, she said she and Teddy had already talked about it. I didn't exactly get the answer I wanted, but I got a practical one."

"I'm curious. What's the practical one?"

"Well, they are waiting, but she says they know college will be a tempting time to explore sexuality. They are not naïve."

"I need to talk with Teddy again."

"Now wait. They agreed that if and when they start having sex, they will be careful. Either condoms or – and I can't believe I'm saying this – Charlie will be on the pill. She asked me if it was okay to get started, just in case."

"What did you say?"

"She's being mature. I told her I would agree, but that was not my permission for having pre-marital sex."

"I think you handled that well. I'm sure the temptation will be there down the road."

"It's just hard thinking of my little girl doing that."

"I'm sure it's hard for all moms. Did you talk to Victor about it?"

"Not yet. I'm debating on whether that should be something I talk to him about it or Charlie and I talk to him together."

"My two cents are that the two of you talk to him. But I'm going at it as how I'd hoped it would be if I had a daughter."

We finished our beers and finished our pizza. Between the two of us, we managed to devour a medium one. I guess we were hungry.

Back at the hotel, we stopped at Kelley's room. I kissed her forehead and gave her a hug.

“Goodnight. We have some sleuthing to do tomorrow.”

“Goodnight, Buck. Sweet dreams and thanks.” She went into her room and shut her door.

In my room, I kicked off my boots and sat back on the bed. Teddy and Charlie Larson, I thought. Theodore and Charlotte Larson. Maybe she would want to keep her maiden name. Many couples were doing that these days.

Chapter 8: The Autopsy

Kelley was obviously up before me. I was still in bed when she knocked. Not that I was still tired. I just knew we had time before our appointment. I opened the door and she stepped past me into the room.

"You're not up yet!"

"We've got a little while before our appointment at the police department."

"Oh, get dressed, lazy bones! Let's go have breakfast."

"I have to shower first."

"Go shower. I'll put on your coffee."

I looked at the hotel coffee. It was a single serve coffeemaker. I guessed that would be okay. Hotel room coffee usually isn't very good.

"Okay. Let me grab my clothes so I can change in the bathroom."

"Chicken!" Her comment made me look at her daringly. She took the hint. "Okay, take your clothes."

After showering, Kelley had two cups of coffee ready and the local news on the television set. There wasn't much of importance airing other than the weather report. I drank my coffee listening to the weather person garble the morning report. I wasn't sure if it was going to rain or not this morning. Maybe the weatherman was under the weather.

"Buck, have you ever been to an autopsy?"

"Yes, but we're not going to an actual autopsy. We are just seeing the report, pictures, and lab results. The autopsy has already been performed."

"I know. I was just curious. I've never been to one. I've been told that the smell can be what gets to you more than the sight of things."

"The smell can be bad but the sight can be a little bit gory if you're not used to it or don't know what to expect. This is a little strange for conversation just before going to eat, though."

"I guess so. Where do you want to go eat breakfast?"

"Cross-Eyed Cricket."

"What? Are you kidding me?"

"Nope. You'll like it."

We walked to the Cross-eyed Cricket. They specialize in breakfast. We got a table and started off with some good coffee.

"I don't know how you find these … unique places."

"Word of mouth. A little research. Not settling for the hum-drum. Willing to try new things."

"Okay, Mr. Excitement! I should know better."

"I don't think you're really complaining."

Kelley shook her head no just as our food arrived. Breakfast was hot and smelling fantastic. It was a hardy way to start the day. Kelley was already taking a bite of her breakfast waffle.

After breakfast, we arrived at the Evansville Police Department and talked to the Desk Sergeant. He had us sit down while he called the officer in charge. We didn't have to wait long.

The officer in charge of the case was a veteran officer by the name of Randall Scobe. He greeted us with a smile.

"Buck Larson. I've heard of you. Understand you're doing some good over in Mount Vernon. Sorry about Dawn. She was a good officer."

"Thanks. And I appreciate your cooperation in this."

"Hey, I've been at this long enough to know that we don't always get it right. If this isn't an accident, I want to know as well. But frankly, I don't see anything to change my opinion. I know the wife was unhappy with her husband, but that doesn't equate to murder."

"I know. I agreed to look into it for a friend and the insurance company."

Scobe took us back to an office and spread out a file to look at. The file was fairly thin. There was the interview of the husband, the officer's final report, the autopsy report which include the lab results, and some crime scene photos. The gin bottle, glass, tonic water, ice bucket, tongs, cherry and peach pits, and a small dinner plate had been taken into evidence and logged on the evidence sheet. It was very thorough.

I looked at the forms. Kelley asked the officer a couple questions.

"Officer Scobe, if it were a murder – hypothetically – is there anything there that might be used to hide the murder?"

"That's an interesting way of looking at. I really have never thought about something that way." He thought for a second. "I don't think so. Both bottles tested negative for cyanide. You really couldn't get rid of the traces unless you replaced the bottles. I suppose a murderer who was really smart could make the switch, but there is nothing to suggest it. And why leave the glass which did have cyanide in it?"

"I hadn't thought about switching out the bottles. Granted, there is no evidence that someone did that, but it is a possibility."

Scobe smiled. Kelley was complimenting his reasoning. "Well, I hadn't thought about it before, either."

I interrupted. "Randall, can we get copies of the file?"

"Sure, but there is a copy fee. There aren't many sheets here, so you probably are looking at less than five dollars. And by the way, it's Randy. I never use my full first name."

"Thanks, Randy. We don't mind paying."

Randy got up with the file and went to the front desk.

"I guess I expected a little more resistance, Buck. Are most police officers as amenable to cases being looked at?"

"Randy is a veteran officer so he's not threatened by a case being reviewed. A lot of officers see outside review as way to 'catch' them making mistakes. It comes from preparing to testify in court and everything they do coming under scrutiny."

"I guess it can develop a sense of being persecuted."

Randy came back in with a file for us. "You can pay at the front desk. It's $3.45. Hey, let me know if you come up with something that shows it was anything but an accidental death. New evidence can open a case."

"Thanks, Randy."

We paid the fee up at the front desk and headed out into the sunshine. The day was shaping up nicely.

"What now, Buck?"

"Let's head back to the hotel and look over this report. We can also call Kevin Hayes and set up an appointment. He's probably expecting to hear from us so he can get the insurance money. I'm curious what he will have to say."

Back at the hotel, we spread out the papers on a coffee table in my room.

"We're missing something." Kelley kept looking at the reports.

"I agree, but what?"

"Let me keep looking. Why don't you call Mr. Hayes and set up an appointment?"

Kelley looked over the papers again as I called Kevin Hayes. I set up a meeting for the next morning and then had another idea. I got ahold of a Stanford Ellington and arranged to meet with him at his home that afternoon.

"Kelley, I've got a meeting for us with the silent partner."

"Stanford Ellington? That's great. I wonder what he thinks of all this?"

Stanford Ellington's house sat outside Evansville in Newburgh.

Newburgh started as a separate town but had grown into a wealthy suburb of Evansville. The Ellington house appeared as a two-story Colonial near the Ohio River.

Mr. Ellington looked just as I pictured him. Grey hair at his sides, but with a full head of hair. He stood about 6'1" and looked like he weighed about 190 lbs. He had a bushy mustache that matched his bushy eyebrows. He answered the door in tan khakis and a light green knit pullover with the Polo design. No socks. He wore deck shoes like he was ready to board his yacht.

"Good afternoon, Mr. Larson. Please come in. And who is your lovely companion?"

"This is Dr. Morgan. She's my partner."

"I should be so lucky to have such an attractive business partner. Please, come on in."

Kelley smiled and replied, "Thank you."

"May I offer you some tea?" Before we could answer, Mr. Ellington rang a bell and a well-dressed servant entered with a tray of tea and English biscuits – what we Americans call cookies.

The gentleman servant poured Mr. Ellington his tea and then looked to Kelley questioningly.

"Just tea, thank you."

The man nodded and poured before finally looking at me.

"None for me, thank you."

Again, he nodded and then turned to Mr. Ellington. "Will there be anything else, Sir?"

"Not right now, Geoffrey. Thank you very much." Mr. Ellington watched Geoffrey leave and then addressed us. "What can I do for you two?"

Kelley began the questions sensing that Stanford was a bit smitten with her. "We are looking into the circumstances behind the death of Mrs. Hayes."

"Yes, very sad. She was a nice, but very serious lady."

"Can you tell me a little about the business partnership the three of you had?"

"Well, I'm very interested in developing local companies. Mr. Hayes asked me if I would like to invest in the company many years ago. I think we were at a Chamber of Commerce event where I spoke of needing to invest in local businesses."

"So, he approached you about investing?"

"Yes. I did a little research. The company at the time was somewhat profitable, but one could tell that it could go one way or the other. I started out with a 1/10th share of the company. I insisted that they fully incorporate and have shares as part of the investment. They were set up as a partnership before that."

"A partnership between Mr. Hayes and his wife?"

"Legally. But it was more of a partnership between their families. Eventually, I bought additional shares equally from Mr. and Mrs. Hayes so that we became 1/3 partners each."

"Was there a particular reason you wanted that kind of balance?"

"You are very perceptive young lady. Yes, it was to maintain a balance."

"What a minute?" I interjected. "Didn't that leave the balance with Mr. and Mrs. Hayes?"

"Under most circumstances, yes. But I found that Mrs. Hayes had a better business sense than did her husband although she didn't push her ideas on him. I wish she would have."

Kelley took the questioning back over. "I was under the impression you were a silent partner."

"We certainly wanted to have a single face for the company, but I wasn't totally silent. Neither was Mrs. Hayes, although she worked hard to do things in a way that her husband could save face. Or feel in charge. I think he needed to feel in charge. It was partly why he was made the face of the company."

"So, how do you feel about the current distribution of power?"

Ellington laughed. "As you can imagine. I will try to buy up to have a 50% share or, if I can't, I'll try to sell out my portion of the company."

"Do you think Mr. Hayes is capable of harming his wife?"

"Now, that's the crux of your visit, isn't it? Honestly, I have a hard time thinking he'd do anything, but probably not for the reasons you would think."

"So, why did you think he wouldn't?"

"He's lazy. Plain and simple."

Kelley looked at me to see if I had anymore questions. I thought she covered everything.

"I want to thank you for your time Mr. Ellington. You've been very helpful and a wonderful host."

"I'd be delighted, Dr. Morgan, if you'd allow me to host you socially sometime."

Kelley blushed. "I'm flattered but I'm married."

Stanford looked at me. "I didn't realize."

"Oh, not to him." Kelley then looked at me apologetically.

"It was a pleasure Dr. Morgan." He turned to me. "And to meet you as well, Mr. Larson."

"Likewise," I replied.

We walked back to the car. Kelley was still bright red.

"Buck, I … Well, I didn't mean that to come out as it did. You know how I feel about you."

I started to milk that, but I could tell she was deeply troubled about how it came out. "Kelley, it is the truth and I believe you were taken off guard by his advance."

"I was. I never thought I'd be asked out on a date while interviewing the person. I wasn't prepared."

"You were absolutely prepared to do the questioning for our investigation, though."

The change in topic was a relief for Kelley. "I thought it was interesting his take on the business and Mr. Hayes."

"I agree, but I'm not sure how it might help us in this case."

"Motive."

"What motive?"

"Don't you find it odd that the company needed outside investment in the first place?"

"No, not really."

"I think the company was losing money and that Mr. Hayes was hiding that fact from Mrs. Hayes. I believe Mrs. Hayes was under the impression that Mr. Ellington had approached them about investing."

"So, the motive would be either to hide the losses or to maximize what he got from the company."

"Yes, I would think so."

"If it's to hide the losses, he'd still have Mr. Ellington to deal with and he doesn't impress me as one who is easily hoodwinked."

"No. But it is a possible start."

We got back to the hotel and started looking over the file we were developing. We were sifting through it when Kelley's phone rang. It was her daughter, Charlie.

She picked up and walked away from the table to talk. I continued looking through the file. Kelley came back and joined me in looking at the files.

"Is everything okay?"

"Charlie is getting some scholarship offers. She and Patrick want to go out to my folks for a couple nights. She says it's because her dad can't cook very well. I believe her exact words were Dad's cooking is awful."

"What does Victor say?"

"Apparently he told them to ask me. Strange."

"Do you need to head back? I can always get a rental car when done here or I can come back if you need me to ride with you."

"Don't be silly. I'm sure it's just a little frustrating for him. Quite honestly, he's not a very good chef; not even at grilling. I kind of thought that they'd go out to eat. But I appreciate the offer, Buck."

"Let's take a break from this. Might help our brains."

"What do you have in mind?"

"How about a little sightseeing? We could head out to Angel Mounds and walk around."

"Ah, a little hiking. That would do me some good."

We headed out to Angel Mounds Park. The center gave an overview of the Natives that had lived in the area. They were among a group that had built mounds and the park near Evansville was one of several preserved sites. We walked the park grounds and visited the burial mounds. The fresh air gave us a chance to clear our heads as I had hoped it would.

"You up for a fancy dinner tonight?" I asked Kelley.

She smiled. "Of course. What did you have in mind?"

"The Red Geranium."

"Sounds like a flower."

"Very nice restaurant over in New Harmony."

"I accept your date, Sir." She bowed ceremoniously.

After going back to the hotel to change, we were on the road toward New Harmony. The town had been founded and inhabited by two different Utopian groups, the Harmonites and the Rappites. Both groups thought that the end of the world was near, yet each left their mark on the community.

White tablecloths draped over the tables with a candle burning as a centerpiece. Cloth napkins and an array of silverware were aside the bone white plates. Crystal glasses sat awaiting attention from a server dressed in black. New York's finest would be impressed with the ambiance of the restaurant.

We were shown to a table toward the center of the room, yet still gave a sense of privacy. I held a chair out for Kelley as she sat.

"Thank you, kind sir."

I smiled and sat down across from her. The waiter poured out water and took our order. Our salads were brought out and we talked and ate.

We were enjoying ourselves when a woman of about 35 started slapping her table slightly over from us. She motioned to her throat. She was choking and her date seemed paralyzed, staring at her. I jumped up and hustled over.

"Are you choking?" Although it seemed she was, I wanted to make sure I wasn't dealing with a seizure or something else. She nodded so I grabbed her from behind and made an upward thrust below the rib cage. She was still choking, so I did it again, dislodging a cherry from her throat. It had come from the dessert she had been eating. I heard the sudden intake of air. She felt a bit limp as I eased her back into her chair.

"Thank you," she eventually managed to get out.

I moved a strand of hair that was dangling in her face so I could see her face better. "Are you okay?" She nodded again. I looked at her date. "You need to get her to the hospital or a clinic. I think she's fine, but she ought to be checked out just the same."

Kelley had come over and then walked with me back to our table. "Well, you sure know where the excitement is, Buck."

I laughed. "Just trying to impress you with all my skills. How am I doing?" I held her chair out as she sat back down.

"I'll give you a 9 out of 10."

"What does a guy have to do to get a 10 from you?"

Kelley smiled but didn't' say anything more about that. She went back to her salad. She looked up again quickly like she had a though.

"What is it, Kelley?"

"I think I know what was missed, but I'll wait until I can look at the police report again." She took another bite of salad. She had a look that said she was very pleased with herself.

The meal was enjoyable. My steak was perfect and the whipped potatoes were delicious. Kelley had an Italian dish with chicken and a mix of vegetables. We both had crème Brule' for dessert, avoiding the cherry-based dessert. I tried to pay at the end of our meal, but the waiter said that the management insisted it was on the house. I slipped our server a $20 bill and thanked him.

It was late as we got back to the hotel. Kelley insisted on taking the police report to her room and suggested I get some rest after my heroics. I didn't argue at first, but after about an hour and a half of not being able to fall asleep, I walked over to Kelley's room and knocked.

She answered the door. And then had me come in. I must have been staring unconsciously at her.

"Buck, are you okay?"

Kelley had on deep purple, satin pajamas. They were short sleeve and shorts. Her marvelous shape filled the night garments perfectly. Her well-toned legs. Her top buttoned but tantalizingly suggesting the curvy breasts beneath. She looked like a dream. So beautiful. So breathtaking.

"Buck?!"

"I'm sorry. You just look fantastic!"

"Does that mean I don't always look fantastic?"

That kind of shook me. "You always look fine." I shook myself out of my staring at her. "Did you find what you wanted?"

She handed me back the file. "I think I did, but let me mull this over a little. It can wait until after we interview the husband."

I took the file and bid her a goodnight forgetting my original reason for coming over to her room. She smiled and guided me out of her room, closing the door behind me, not even daring a hug. I had gotten an image I couldn't and didn't want to get out of my head. I smiled uncontrollably all the way back to my room.

Chapter 9: Business as Usual

My phone rang waking me up this morning. It was Kelley.

"Is it safe to come over? I wondered if I was going to have to fight you off last night." She paused. "And I wondered if I would fight you off."

"It's safe. And you know I'd never make it so you'd have to fight me off. But it would be dangerous if we were both weak at the moment. If you were willing, well, I'll leave it at that."

"I know, but you sure had a look last night. Scary and, well, rather flattering, too."

I laughed. "I know what you mean. Sorry. I don't think you realize how beautiful, how stunningly beautiful you can be."

"Thank you but don't be sorry. I'll see you in 10 minutes."

We opted for just coffee for breakfast after our rather heavy meals lately. Across the street from the hotel was the Evansville Museum and a little walk along the Ohio River. The cool breeze off the river made for a nice morning stroll.

"Kelley, I was thinking that the police didn't consider the possibility of suicide in their report."

"Hmm, I didn't see anything that suggested it either, though. There wasn't a suicide note. Purposely cracking fruit pits with cyanide in them would be a rather exotic way to commit suicide. It would certainly leave the question open of whether she took her own life or not."

"But maybe that's the point. If there is life insurance and you want to hide a suicide, make it look like an accident. Insurance doesn't pay out on suicides."

"I suppose. But, Buck, I think you're over thinking it."

"Probably. You have something, though, don't you?"

"I do, but like I said, let's wait until after we talk to the husband. What I saw in the report would point toward murder."

We had walked a few miles by the time we got back to the hotel. The conversation had made the walking easy.

"Ready to talk to Mr. Hayes?"

"I believe I am, Buck."

The Hayes home was in the older wealthy neighborhood out by the Evansville Country Club, but we were to meet with Mr. Hayes at his office in the company's building not far from the old Sterling Beer brewery plant in downtown Evansville.

As we pulled up to the building, I could see a convertible Cadillac XLR in the reserved parking spot for Kevin Hayes. I had to laugh a bit. It is a nice car, but it was thought of as Cadillac's attempt to rival the Chevrolet Corvette. They only made them for a few years.

Kelley remarked on the car. "Isn't that a Corvette? Some people claim that it is a symbol of inadequacy; an attempt to compensate. Professionally, I've observed times when that's true and there have been studies conducted."

"Well, it may be, but it's a Cadillac, not a Corvette. Maybe even more of a symbol. I wonder the psychological take on getting a substitute for a macho substitute?"

Mr. Hayes was sitting back in his office looking at his computer screen as we approached. There didn't appear to be a secretary. I knocked on the door jamb as we got to the office.

"Come in," Hayes said as he blanked his screen. "I assume you are Mr. Larson and Dr. Morgan?"

"We are." Kelley and I sat in a couple of chairs in front of Mr. Hayes' desk. "We just have a few questions."

"Certainly. I understand the insurance company hired you to investigate my wife's passing."

We left that presumption without answer. The insurance company would be paying if we came up with something, but we'd get paid either way. It didn't matter to our agency who was the paying entity.

Kelley led off the questioning. "You weren't at home when Mrs. Hayes died. Were you home at all that afternoon or evening?"

"I came home from work – the office here – but went back out almost immediately on the day my wife died. Honestly, we hadn't been getting along that well. I headed out to the club with my friends. We watched some games and played a little poker. I came up a whopping $5.25 ahead."

"Did you see her at all before leaving?"

"I came in the house and changed. She was sitting in the lounge chair there in the den with the t.v. on. I told her I was heading out and she either said okay or nodded. I couldn't say for sure. Like I said, we weren't exactly getting along."

"Was she drinking when you left?"

"I think so. She always had a bottle beside her lately."

"What was she drinking?"

"She generally had a Gin and Tonic in the evening. She liked the taste of it with fruit or cheese she said. I'm more of a whiskey person."

"Did you get her anything? A drink, fruit?"

"No. Just headed out."

"Do you know if she had anything to eat before you left?"

"Not really. She had started eating cucumber sandwiches lately. She picked it up from some British cooking show or BBC Special. I don't really care for them myself. She had bought a bunch of fruit and vegetables from the Farmer's Market lately. Peaches,

Pears, Blackberries, Cherries, asparagus, peas; that kind of stuff."

I took over the questioning. "What time did you get back home from the Club?"

"It was sometime around midnight. I almost went straight upstairs and to bed, but I had stepped into the den just to check to see if any dishes had been left out. I saw her in the chair but didn't realize she was dead until trying to get her to answer me a couple times."

"Was she still in a sitting position?"

"She was, sort of. I came around and saw she was slightly slumped over and had a foam like drool coming out of her mouth."

"What did you do next?"

"I shook her and then called 9-1-1."

"How long did it take for the emergency crew to get there?"

"I'm not sure. It seemed forever but the operator kept me on the phone. It was probably only 5 minutes, but I don't know."

"Mr. Hayes, did Vicky ever talk about killing herself or anything along that line?"

"No. I mean we weren't getting along, but it wasn't that bad. She was a little down. If she were thinking along those lines, she would have said something to her best friend, Jackie but I sure don't think that she would do something like kill herself. I understand insurance companies checking things out, but this was just an accident."

"What about the company here? How is it doing? Why have Mr. Ellington invest in the company?"

"Ellington wanted to help local businesses, so he asked to invest in our business. We were doing well, and it was understood he was investing with an idea of taking a share of the profit. I still manage the company."

"So Ellington approached you about investing in your company?"

"Yes. We were at a Chamber of Commerce event where he was speaking. He came up asking about investing in the company after his talk."

"You'll control two-thirds of the shares now. What if Ellington wants to buy enough to balance the control between the two of you?"

"Well, that would be company business, Mr. Larson. I'm not sure that you or the insurance company need insight to my business plans. I don't think that is relevant to your investigation."

"Possibly not. Possibly the financial aspect of the company could come into play."

"I'm not sure what you're suggesting, Mr. Larson, but I don't like it. I believe this interview is over now. I've answered your questions regarding my wife's death. I've been tolerant as much as I'm willing regarding the company. I'm sure you can show yourself the way out."

"Just one more thing, Mr. Hayes," Kelley interjected.

"Of course, Dr. Morgan." Kevin Hayes seemed relieved at the moment to be talking to Kelley now.

"How did Mrs. Hayes take her GTs? Straight or on-the-rocks?"

He looked at her hard. "She generally had ice with her drink." He turned cold quickly. "Now, good day to the both of you."

We left. Obviously Mr. Hayes had not been pleased with our final line of questioning.

"Well, Kelley, did you get what you wanted?"

"Not sure if I wanted it, but I'm pretty sure he murdered her, now. I think I know how."

"I felt like that. He certainly lied about the investment with the company. I think we should take what we have to Jackie and get her input on all of this. She's the one hiring us, plus she is an attorney."

Chapter 10: Accident, Suicide or Murder

I called Jackie to tell her we were coming over and asked her to set aside some time to go over the findings so far. She cleared her afternoon to go over the case with us.

"Buck, I'm beginning to enjoy this detective business with you. It is exciting putting the pieces together."

"Well, it's mainly you putting the pieces together so far on this one. I have a feeling, but you seem to have pieced the puzzle together. I can't wait to hear what you have."

"So it's okay to wait until we get to Jackie's for me to reveal what I see? You don't have a macho need to have it given to you first?"

"I don't need the credit. And I know I can still learn some things. No, I don't need to be falsely validated."

"You're not the usual male, Buck."

"I'm going to take that as a compliment."

In presenting our findings to Jackie, we weren't really going to need an extra night in Evansville, even as nice as it had been. We checked out and loaded up Kelley's Jaguar to head over to Mt. Vernon.

I had her stop to pick up some local wine as we headed over. Kauffman Winery had some inexpensive, sweet wines and I grabbed a bottle of red. The clerk recommended Zap's Tavern which was nearby and said we could grab lunch there. So we took a little detour down St. Phillip's Road to grab some bar food.

We both ordered burgers and fries. The lunch crowd was starting to pick up so I was glad we got in ahead of it.

"So what's with the wine?"

"I thought we could celebrate our second case later. We ought to make a tradition of picking up something to commemorate our adventures."

"That little souvenir won't be around long."

"No, but it will be part of the memory."

"Buck, you can be a strange one."

We ate our lunch and then continued on into Mt. Vernon. The afternoon was starting to get hot and muggy. The humidity was thick in a town that basically sits near the convergence of the Ohio and Wabash

Rivers. Across the Ohio lay Kentucky and across the Wabash was Illinois.

Inside The McFadden Law Office, Jackie was eager to hear what we had come up with. I spread out our file on a conference table.

"Mr. Hayes is certainly in denial, if not just lying, about the financial stability of his company. He tried to make it seem that Mr. Ellington wanted in on his company although Kevin was trying to bring in needed cash."

"Does the company have an accountant?" Jackie asked.

"It appears that Mr. Hayes does not have a secretary and manages his own books. Not a smart way to run a company. I also floated out the idea of suicide. Of course, suicide would eliminate the paying out of a life insurance policy. He didn't think it was something she would do."

"Well, suicide wasn't really something I think she'd consider. She wasn't the type."

Kelley pointed to the autopsy report. "See here where they list stomach contents."

Both Jackie and I looked. "I don't see anything unusual," Jackie said and then looked up at Kelley.

"Aside from the cyanide, what do you see?"

"Makings of a cucumber sandwich. Gin. Tonic water." I listed what I saw.

Kelley smiled. "But where are the pieces of cherries and peaches?"

Jackie looked down again before looking up. "There isn't any."

"So she couldn't have accidentally poisoned herself with something she didn't eat."

I looked over at Kelley impressed. She smiled back.

Jackie looked through the papers again. "It's so plain, but we all missed it. Good job, Kelley. But how did someone get the cyanide in then? The gin bottle and the tonic water were clean."

I now understood Kelley's question about whether she took her drinks on the rocks or plain. "Kelley, you figured out that he had the cyanide in the ice. It came out as the gin melted the ice cubes."

"Exactly. Now we need to have the police lab check for cyanide on the ice tongs and in the ice bucket."

Jackie shook her head. "They have enough now to at least question Kevin. My guess is he'll break when the evidence is presented. Let me call the police to have them do the testing."

While Jackie called, I turned to Kelley. "See! We make a good team. That was some great deductive reasoning."

"Beginners luck," she replied. But I could tell she was pleased, as well she should be.

Jackie hung up the phone. "I talked to Officer Scobe. He says he will have the lab run the tests right away and give me a call back. He is quite impressed with the catch on the absence of the cherries and peaches."

"Well, and hopefully the insurance company will pay our bill so you're not stuck with it," I added.

"Buck, I'll be happy to pay although, yes, it would be good if the insurance company would cover the costs. You going to give me an invoice?"

"Sure. Daily rate and hotel rooms. It won't be too bad."

"By the way, Scobe asked that you hang around to fill out a report. And he says he owes you guys lunch."

Kelley tapped me on my shoulder. "Hey Genius, we checked out of our rooms. Where do you want to stay? I guess we could check back in."

"We can stay at the house here."

"Are you sure? You seemed a bit funny about it."

"I'm probably always going to be a bit funny about it, but I need to get over it."

Jackie laughed. "You two are welcome to come down to the waterfront this evening. They are having a community concert in the park. We can grab some beers at the American Legion afterwards."

I looked at Kelley. She nodded. "Sounds good. We're in."

We left Jackie's office and drove over to my house on Main Street. Kelley parked by the carriage house garage again and we grabbed our bags and went inside. I put Kelley's bag upstairs in the bedroom, leaving mine downstairs by the couch.

"Are you going to sleep on the couch?"

"That's my plan. I don't mind."

"Why don't you sleep in the bedroom? If you can behave yourself, it won't be a problem."

"I don't know."

"I won't wear the purple pajamas." She laughed. "Can't have you going all crazy."

"We can talk about it later. Shall we celebrate another case done?" I held up the wine I had just bought.

"Sure. But isn't that going to be a little warm?"

I touched the bottle. It was a little warm. I looked in the refrigerator. There was a bottle of rose' on the shelf. It, too, was from the Kauffman Winery.

"Rose'?"

"Yes, please."

I poured out a couple glasses and we sat on the couch. Kelley sipped her wine and nodded.

"It's not bad, is it?"

"No, not at all, Buck."

"What do you think the kids are up to?"

"Well, my mom is spoiling my two. I hesitate to think what my daughter and your son are up to."

"They're good kids. Have you heard from Victor?"

"Not really. He must be in a mood. Probably upset that the kids wanted to get away from his cooking and wanted to go to my mom's house. I won't let him put me in a bad mood."

"How's Danae doing holding down the sessions on her own?"

"Danae is ready for me to be back, but she says that she is managing. She texted earlier. I hope we don't have too many out-of-town cases, but it is nice once-in-a-while."

"Hey, maybe we will get an exotic location eventually."

"You mean like Saint Lucia?"

"I offered to have you come along."

"I know. Probably should have."

We chatted about everything and nothing, and drank wine for a bit before deciding to head down to the waterfront. It wasn't too far of a walk and as it approached evening, it cooled a bit.

Walking along we could see the old Alexandria Public Library building at the edge of the downtown business district. The old buildings were reminders of a time before malls, bypasses, and big highways. Where a bank now sat used to be a small, local department store. There was a Five and Dime called Tressler's once along the street where the building was now unoccupied, ready to crumble. Another bank, an older one, sat across the street. Drug stores, now shells, and little restaurants had been converted to bars and hardware stores and to the next little shop that dared to give commerce a try. Sad reminders of a time when communities were self-reliant and self-contained.

The courthouse sat in the middle of it all. A town square that still had its old limestone post office. The old buildings around it showed a county seat that once had some prominence. Down by the river, improvements to the park and an apartment renewal promised a chance at new prosperity. I hoped that the foundation I ran there would help pump new life into the town. It was slow going. The sister city project I led was starting to show some dividends within both communities.

People greeted us as we headed toward the park. As we neared, we could see the Ohio River rolling past the town. The river waters moving deceptively quick. A few boats were out on the water. Most people at the park had lawn chairs they had set up, getting ready for the concert. Kids played on the playground equipment scattered around the bandstand. Kelley saw Jackie who waved us over to join her and her daughter, Beth.

"Hey, Jackie." I called out as we got by them. Jackie had a blanket spread out.

"You two are welcome to join us."

"Thanks," Kelley said and then turned to Beth. "You must be the fabulous volleyball player I've heard about."

Beth grinned shyly. "Oh, I don't know about that, but I'm Beth. Pleased to meet you. You must be Buck's girlfriend."

I chuckled. Kelley looked lost for a second then responded. "I'm his partner in the detective agency. I have a daughter about your age who may get a basketball scholarship to play in college. I understand you'll be off to Bloomington to play at Indiana."

"I want to get my law degree. Indiana is a great place for pre-Law. Maybe I'll get accepted to law school there, too."

"I thought you might do Harvard Law," I threw into the conversation.

"Maybe. That's a few years off and a long way away."

We settled down to listen to the local band. They played a lot of the summer bandstand staples such as marches, but also had some jazz numbers as well. There was something about a band playing in the park by the river on a summer evening.

As the concert wrapped up, a couple of girls from Beth's school team joined her and asked her to hang out with them. Jackie gave her nod, but told Beth to be home by midnight.

The three of us started walking up to the Legion.

"Didn't you drive?" I asked Jackie.

"I did, but I parked by the Legion since we had agreed to go there after the concert. I take it you walked down?"

I nodded and Kelley responded. "It's nice getting out and walking."

We walked into the Legion. Randy was at the bar.

"Hey, Randy!"

"Hey, Buck! Long time, no see. Looks like you have two beautiful ladies this time. Next it will be three. Corona?"

"You bet!" I turned to the ladies. "What would you two like?"

They both said Corona was fine.

"Randy, make it 3 please."

"Coming up!"

We sat at an open table. There was a ballgame playing on the t.v. I remembered back some years when I watched a Chicago Cubs game there with Dawn. Sure enough, the Cubs were on the tube. This time they were playing the White Sox. A pure Chicago match-up. Randy brought over the 3 beers.

"I'll start a tab for you. It's good to see you, Buck."

"You, too, Randy."

"So, Kelley, what clued you in on the missing food?" Jackie was curious.

"Well, Buck and I kept saying we were missing something. It dawn on me that we weren't missing something, the report was missing something. If it was cherries and peaches that poisoned her, then they had to be there."

"So what made you think the cyanide was in the ice?"

"It wasn't in the bottles, and it would be too obvious if it were a white powder in the bottom of a glass. That's why I asked if she took her drink on the rocks. Kevin wouldn't want to lie about it because someone like you would counter it. So he simply stated the truth, that she took it on the rocks and hoped no one would think about the poison being frozen into the ice. I think he realized the track I was on by the end."

"By the way, Scobe called just before I got to the park The lab confirms cyanide on the tongs and in the ice bucket. They are heading out to question Kevin. Honestly, it will still be tough proving he did it unless they can get him to confess."

"Or they find the real source of the cyanide," I added. "I think Scobe will start checking around to see who sells the stuff and see if they can tie a purchase to Mr. Hayes."

"Is that hard to do?" Kelley asked.

"Not once they can narrow it down. I'm going to guess Kevin cracks though. He didn't handle your questions well. I think he probably will think he's done for anyway."

Jackie lifted her bottle. "Cheers!"

"Cheers!" Kelley and I replied.

Our bottles clanked and we finished off the beer, so I ordered another round.

"I hope this isn't going to appear on your expense report," Jackie chided.

"Maybe."

It was getting close to midnight when Jackie's phone rang. "It's probably Beth," Jackie remarked as she fumbled with her phone. "Hello?"

Jackie nodded a few times and then hung up after offering Thanks to the caller. "That was Officer Scobe. Kevin Hayes confessed to it all."

"That makes things easier," I mused.

"Indeed." Jackie yawned. "I'm suddenly tired. Can I give you two a ride?"

"Yes, thanks." I think Kelley was done walking for the day. She seemed happy to have the ride.

I paid the bill and told Randy again that it was good to see him. We shook hands and then I headed out to Jackie's car with Kelley and Jackie. I got in the back and let Kelley have the front seat.

"Where to?" Jackie asked.

"My house, please."

As Jackie pulled up, she looked at me. "Thanks again, Buck. I appreciate it."

I smiled. "You're welcome, but it was mainly Kelley this time."

Jackie smiled at Kelley. "I know. Thanks, Kelley. Take care of our guy here." With that she motored off home.

I bowed to Kelley as we stood on the sidewalk and indicated the house. "Shall we?"

"We shall." Kelley took my elbow and we walked up to the house. I unlocked and we went in feeling satisfied and tired.

"I'm going to go up and change. I'll yell down when it's okay for you to come up."

"Kelley, are you sure?"

"I think I can control you."

"I am tired. I don't think it would take much to control me."

Kelley went up and after about 5 minutes called down. "It's okay now."

I went up. She had on an old sweatshirt with the sleeves cut short with a pair of athletic shorts. She twirled around once. "Sufficiently, unattractive?"

"No. You are still very attractive. Maybe more so, but it doesn't come across as seductive, so there's that."

"I'll take it. Now, get ready for bed. I'm tired and want to get to sleep."

I changed into my pajama pants and left a t-shirt on. Kelley was already asleep when I came to bed. That made me smile. I crawled into bed beside her and put an arm around her. She unconsciously scooted up against me, her back to my front. It was a restful night. I slept very well.

Chapter 11: Insurance

I woke up with my arms around Kelley and her back right up against me. She was still sleeping, so I tried to slip out of bed without waking her. My first attempt resulted in her grabbing my arm and holding it to her. She mumbled something but didn't wake. I was able to slowly get up on my second attempt although I wasn't sure I wanted to.

Downstairs, I started some breakfast for us. I microwaved some bacon and got some eggs and toast going. One of these days I'd go ahead and make Eggs Benedict. It was nice to cook up what some perceived as a fancy breakfast. I had coffee pods ready to put in. The single cup coffeemaker was becoming one of my favorite innovations.

I could hear Kelley coming down the stairs, so I popped in the first coffee. It was brewing when she reached the kitchen.

"Morning, Handsome!"

"Good morning, Beautiful! Ready for some breakfast?"

"Would love some. See! We managed to behave, and you didn't have to sleep on the couch. You would have been miserable."

"It was much nicer. Yes, we managed. I'm sure being tired had a lot to do with it. But the bed was definitely more comfortable."

We sat down and had our eggs and bacon with some toast and coffee. I turned on the television to get the local news. The report of Kevin Hayes being charged with the murder of his wife was the lead. Officer Scobe was interviewed, giving credit for assistance to the Morelli and Larson Detective Agency. I hadn't thought about the publicity.

Jackie called. "Buck, I hope you're watching the news. The Evansville Police gave you and Kelley credit for solving the case."

"Scobe is a good guy. I appreciate it."

"Ellington asked for your number. I thought I should give you a heads-up."

"Interesting. I wonder what he wants."

"Well, honestly, I think he is more interested in Kelley. He wanted to see if she was really married.

Curious about your relationship with her. But also about the case. I guess he has some questions for the business."

"I'll give Kelley a heads-up." Kelley heard that and looked over questioningly. "Take care, Jackie."

"What was that about giving me a heads-up?"

"Apparently Ellington is still interested in you and seeing if he was getting a line from you about being married. Plus, he has some questions about the case."

"Seriously? I seem to attract the nut cases."

"Hey! I take offense."

"You're the nuttiest one of all, but for some reason I like you." She came over and gave me a reassuring hug. I started to kiss her but stopped myself.

"Do you want to shower and dress first?"

"Definitely." With that, Kelley headed back upstairs. I heard the shower start after a bit and could hear her singing a little while washing up.

The phone rang again. I didn't recognize the number but I answered anyway. "Hello?"

"Mr. Larson? This is Stanford Ellington."

"What can I do for you, Mr. Ellington?"

"Well, I guess on a personal level, not much. I must admit that I find Dr. Morgan quite thrilling."

"I can't speak for her, but she is married and I don't think she's interested in an affair."

"Sounds like you know, but I'm not prying there. I do have some questions that relate to my business investment."

"Go ahead. I'll answer if I can."

"I need to know how to proceed with the company and want to take action before Mr. Hayes goes to court. Perchance, did you discover any irregularities with the company finances?"

"We didn't get into the finances specifically, but there are certainly indicators that the company isn't doing well. Hayes kept his own books which we know is a bad practice. The potential for skimming the books was there. I don't know about audits. You should have a better idea."

"I think I was too silent a partner. Thanks, I think I'll have an attorney get on to seizing company assets so he doesn't tie them up in court."

"I wish you luck, Mr. Ellington."

"Thank you. Give my best to Dr. Morgan when you see her."

"I will." I turned around and Kelley was there.

"Your turn. Who were you talking to, by the way?"

"One of your many admirers."

"Oh, Ellington. What did he want?"

"You. But he also wanted some information regarding the company. I think he might be in a legal battle about his investment."

"That's sad." She paused. "Well, go get dressed!"

I went upstairs and showered and then dressed. I actually felt comfortable here in the house for the first time since Dawn had been killed.

I was thinking that she and Kelley would have really gotten along.

I brought the bags downstairs and hung the towels in the basement by the washer. The lady who came in to clean once a week would throw them in a load. She really helped keep things up. Kelley had cleaned up the kitchen and had put away the dried dishes.

"You know, Buck. We work together well in a lot of ways." She smiled her smile. Despite the situations we were in, we had become the best of friends. "Where to next?"

"I guess we need to give Officer Scobe our statements and then we head home."

We drove over to Evansville and meet with Scobe at the police station. He took our statements and we signed them.

"Ready for lunch? I owe you two."

"You don't have to."

"But I want to. Let's go over to Franco's. You guys like Italian?"

Kelley nodded. I replied, "You bet."

We sat down at Franco's Italian Food. The waitress came over to take our order.

"Randy! You haven't been by in awhile. What's the matter?"

"I was just here last week. You know I love this place."

"Ah, that's good. Who are your friends?"

"This is the couple that solved the Hayes murder case."

"They look like a lovely couple. What are you going to have?"

Kelley looked at Scobe. "What do you suggest?"

"I always get the special. It changes from week to week, but it's always good."

"I'll have the special, too."

"I'll make it easy, then," I added. "Make it 3 specials."

The meal was delicious. We avoided talking about the case too much, but I was curious.

"Do you think the D.A. will need us to testify?"

"Hayes confessed. Unless he pleads not guilty then I doubt it. Oh, but the insurance company asked for a copy of the report and wanted to talk to you. I told them I'd pass along the message, but wasn't sure if you wanted me handing out your number, so I didn't."

Scobe handed me the insurance agency's card. I took it.

"Not sure if we are going to get out of here today, Kelley."

"Well, at least we have a place to stay if we have to."

We got back to the police station and said goodbye to Scobe. I called the number of the insurance agency. A gentleman answered. "Foremost Insurance, Jeffrey Albertson speaking."

"Mr. Albertson, I was asked to call you. This is Buck Larson and I have Dr. Morgan with me."

"Asked to call?"

"We are the Morelli and Larson Detective Agency."

"Oh, yes. Thank you! I was wondering if you could come by my office? We are out on Division."

"Sure. When?"

"Now if you have the time."

"We'll be right over."

Kelley shook her head. "Another interview?"

"That's how we get paid, Darling."

Kelley drove us out to the office address and we went in the front lobby. It was a big executive office complex. I asked the secretary for the Foremost Insurance Office and she pointed us down the hall.

Mr. Albertson greeted us as we came in. "It's wonderful to meet you. We appreciate the work you did on this."

"Well, thank you, Mr. Albertson. Let me introduce my partner and the person who really solved this, Dr. Morgan."

Albertson reached out to shake Kelley's hand.

"I've got the statements from the police. I just needed some signatures." He pushed a paper toward us along with an envelope.

"What's this?" I asked. "We haven't submitted our bill for working this case yet."

"Oh, your bill will be paid. There is a small reward on top of that for saving the company money. Mr. Hayes had a two-million dollar policy on his wife."

"That's a big policy," Kelley remarked.

"Indeed, Ma'am." Albertson pushed the envelope toward Kelley. She opened it. She whistled.

"Buck, there is a check for $200,000 here."

I looked at the form we were signing. It obligated us to testify and provide documentation if the loss denial was challenged in court or related proceedings. We signed.

"Well, thank you, Mr. Albertson. I'll leave our card should you need us to testify."

"Thank you again, Mr. Larson. Dr. Morgan."

We walked out of the office with a $200,000 check. Our bill would barely total $10,000 for the work we did. The detective agency was certainly off to a good start.

"I guess you'll have to have Tina deposit that in our account."

"She's going to be surprised."

It was a cheery ride back to Eudora. Our second case and quite the payoff for it. Kelley dropped me off at my house.

"I need to check at home. Victor seems grumpy. The kids are coming back from my mom's tomorrow."

"I'll pop over to the office tomorrow. I have a couple things to do in Lawrence anyway."

"Okay. See you tomorrow."

Even though it was getting late, I called Ed to see what I missed in Eudora. He told me to come on over so it was off to Ed's I went.

Ed's wife, Erin, met me at the door. "You know he's been grumpy the whole time you've been gone." She gave me a hug and a kiss on the cheek. "I think he's jealous that he's not part of your detective agency. I told him he just doesn't have the legs Kelley does."

"Oh, you're a big help."

We walked through the house and out back onto the patio.

"Well, Stranger, how ya doing?"

"I'm good, Ed. You?"

"Just peachy!"

Erin snorted. "Peachy!"

"Oh, couple of kids acting up around town. Minor stuff. I hear you and your partner solved a big murder case. Made the news, again."

"Kelley did the intellectual heavy lifting on this one. Paid pretty good, too."

"How much?"

"We made over $200,000 on this one."

"What the hell?!"

"Guy had a two-million dollar policy out on his wife. We ended up saving the insurance company that dough and they pay a percentage."

"That's the kind of luck you have."

Erin sat down. "So how are things going with Kelley?"

"In what way, Erin?"

"You know what way."

"She's married. We are good friends, in fact, very close, but not in a romantic relationship."

"She's right for you, Buck."

"I agree, except she's married."

Erin turned to Ed. "You ought to tell him."

I turned to Ed. "Tell me what?"

"Oh hell. Erin and I went over to that Argosy casino in Kansas City a couple nights ago. We had a little playing around money."

Erin laughed. "Forty bucks a piece."

"Stop interrupting. Anyway, we saw Victor over there. I don't know him that well, so at first, I just thought it was a fellow who looked like him. Then he spied us and made sure he had his back to us the rest of the evening. I wasn't sure until when we were heading out and one of the people there called him by name."

"Hmmm. I wonder if he will admit it to Kelley?"

Erin looked at me. "You need to tell her."

"I'm the last one who should tell her."

Ed was surprised. "What do you mean?"

"You two know how I feel about Kelley. Kelley knows how I feel about Kelley. I can't be the one that tells her. It will appear that I'm trying to break them up and I am not. What happens between me and Kelley has to be without a shadow of impropriety. At least it can't be my being involved in breaking them up."

"What if she discovers you knew and didn't say anything?"

"Then she'll know I wouldn't use information to get what I want. She'll know that I value her and her happiness."

Erin touched my shoulder. "Buck, she's not happy now."

"Erin, you know what I mean. It can't be me. If she finds out, she finds out on her own."

"Okay, Buck. I understand. You're a better person than most."

We drank a couple beers, but the weight hanging over us never lifted. It had become a somber evening. I walked home slowly.

I got ready for bed and rested myself with my head on the pillows. Staring at the ceiling, I reminded myself that I was the unlucky at love guy. There was always something. Even when I accepted that I would be in a beautiful yet non-sexual relationship, it got screwed up. I eventually fell asleep, but it wasn't a good sleep.

The next morning, I started to brace myself for going into the office. I debated calling and giving Tina the information she needed. Kelley had the check for Tina to deposit. But I had said I was going in, so I did.

I jumped on the Harley giving her a nice rubdown. Then it was off and into Lawrence. I pulled into the garage off of New Hampshire to park in the motorcycle area. Kelley's Jaguar was in her usual spot near the bikes. I started to walk past, but Kelley was still in her car. I tapped on her window, startling her.

"Oh, Hi Buck!" It was a weak hello.

"What's the matter?"

"I'm not sure I want to say right now."

"Can I walk you up to the office?"

"Yes, I guess I need to go in."

As we headed up, she turned to me before we went in. "He's gambling again. He says the stress of me taking off on this new job and the kids abandoning him to go to my mother's was too much."

I nodded and rubbed her shoulder. I just wanted to listen. Wanted to let her vent what she needed. She didn't say anything for a while.

"How did you respond?"

"I cried. I couldn't say anything. Thank God the kids weren't there yet."

"Let me get Tina started on our files and let's grab some coffee over at Milton's"

Tina handed me the file along with the check. I took them into Tina and explained we were getting a coffee to go over some final points. Tina gave me a look, but didn't say anything. I handed her the check and asked her to deposit it in the agency account. As she stared at the check, I told her we'd be back in a few minutes.

Kelley and I walked over to Milton's. I ordered a couple of coffees and we sat down in the outside courtyard. I set her coffee in front of her.

"Buck, he's gambling again, but blaming it on me. And on the kids."

"You don't need me to remind you about addictive behaviors. You know that blaming is part of the addiction."

"But, have I become the enabler?"

"You know the answer. You got him to go to therapy and to group. That's not enabling."

"But what I do next is either hurtful or enabling."

"You have to decide that for yourself. I particularly can't decide for you. In reality, no one can. I am going to call Teddy and ask him to bring Charlie and Patrick out to my house so you can have some time.

"I already asked Mom to have them stay another night."

"Okay. Now you have to decide your next step."

"What if I decide to give him another chance?"

"Do you want me to be up front?"

"Totally."

"I will continue to be your friend and I will continue to feel the same way about you."

"But?"

"But I would ask you to go on a specific salary as part of the detective agency to remove you, well your husband, from being able to financially harm our company. I would recommend to you that you suggest the same thing with Danae. That she take over the therapy firm and retain you on a salary. It would be for the same reasons. Do you want me to go on?"

"Yes. I appreciate it."

"I would recommend that Charlie and Patrick have any money they have put into a trust fund with your parents as executors. I would also suggest that your parents be given your house and that a rental agreement be drawn up so that you are not at risk of losing your home. You will need a good attorney for all that and cooperation from Victor who may not give it. I hope I'm not being too brutal, and I hope you don't take this as trying to influence you. I'm being as real as I can be under the circumstances. I know what it's like to love someone who has some big issues. It's hard to know when to give up and you don't want to give up too soon if there is a chance."

"I know what I should do. I've helped people with this. I know that one path is clearly the end and the other path keeps both options. Trying to get them to see that staying beyond just reinforces getting by with the behavior and that eventually, it doesn't really look like there is a path to end it. There really are only two paths from the beginning."

"Do you have clients today?"

"Yes. I put them off too long with our investigation."

"Why don't you see them and go to your mother's to think at the end of the day?"

"Funny. I would have thought you'd have invited me out to your place to think."

"That would not be wise right now. You know you're always welcome, but that isn't what you need right now. Plus, you need to be around your kids. I'll talk to Teddy. He can go one evening without seeing Charlie."

"Buck, what will you tell him?"

"The truth. At least as much as he needs to know. He's going to hear it anyway."

"I guess Charlie would tell him. Thanks."

We finished our coffees and I walked Kelley up to her office. Tina was typing up the file. Kelley went in Danae's office to talk to her.

"Tina, that should help out the detective agency's financial situation."

"I'll say. And you want me to submit the bill for services on top of it?"

"I do."

"You've had two cases and pulled in quiet the chunk of money. I think I got into the wrong profession."

"Maybe, and in these cases, I haven't even been shot at like before."

"Mr. Larson! Don't talk like that!"

"Hey, how is Mr. Dunwiddy? You two seem quite smitten with each other."

Tina blushed. "Danny is very nice. I like him."

"He does seem to be a fine young man."

Kelley came out of Danae's office. She seemed more together. "Good morning, Tina."

"Good morning, Dr. Morgan. Congratulations on solving the murder case."

Kelley laughed. "Thank you. Now it's back to dealing with matters of the mind."

I walked over to Danae's office. She smiled. "Want to come in and talk?"

"I can." She gestured for me to come in.

We sat down. "I guess we tend to give the same advice. At least to Kelley."

"Oh?"

"I had mentioned doing something to protect her finances if she decided to give him another chance."

"This is big. It's not uncommon, I don't think, to backslide on an addiction. I don't know what the cure rate is, but I'm guessing not high."

"Depends on the person. The will to beat it has to be there. My personal opinion, which I did NOT share with Kelley, is it's not."

"I don't know him well enough, but, of course, I'm biased so I won't say."

"Well, you're doing the right things. I know how you feel about her. Letting her know you're her friend regardless helps. Of course, I'm biased, too. I think the two of you should be together, but not like this, right now. How did the case go?"

"Honestly, Kelley was the brains on this one. She figured it out where the police and I didn't see it."

"I think her working this case did her a world of good. Particularly since she got to work it with you."

"Thanks. I guess we'll just have to see where this goes. I'm hoping the publicity lands us a few more cases."

"Well, I know James says he'd hire you again in a minute."

"How is your boyfriend doing?"

"Can you keep a secret? I didn't want to tell Kelley under the circumstances but I have to tell someone."

"I'm dying to know now. What is it?"

"Mr. Gilliford isn't my boyfriend."

"I'm sorry. What happened?"

"He's my fiancé! We're engaged."

"Congratulations! Good luck keeping that one secret. But she won't hear it from me."

"Thanks. I'll only wait a few days to tell her."

"Dr. Cornwall," called Tina as she opened the door, "your first appointment is here."

I stepped out. Kelley came out to greet her first appointment who was sitting waiting. Kelley walked me to the outer door first.

"Thanks, Buck. You're really a friend."

"Call me later to let me know how you are."

"I will." Kelley walked her patient into her office.

I waved at Tina. "Later."

"Goodbye, Mr. Larson."

I got on my Harley to ride. I wondered what our next case would be and whether Kelley would be up to working on it with me. I wouldn't have long to wonder.

A Case of Love Sickness

Chapter 12: Love Hurts

I had just pulled into my garage after having filled up the Harley Duo-Glide and checking her out when the phone rang. I answered a bit disconnectedly.

"Hello? Is anyone there?" I heard someone calling through the phone. It jerked me out of my inattention.

"Sorry. This is Buck Larson."

"Thank you, Mr. Larson. I'm Andy Ruby. I'm a defense attorney over in Kansas City. I was wondering if you'd be available to take a case for my client?"

"Probably. Who's your client?"

"Harold Bowsman. He's been charged with killing his girlfriend, Patty Downset. Well, not really his girlfriend, but someone he had dated for a bit."

"Did he?"

"Murder her? You're very direct. No. He says he had nothing to do with it."

"But there must be some evidence?"

"His gun. Fingerprints. Some messages. If I were the prosecuting attorney, I'd feel good about the evidence I had. But I believe my client. I don't think he did it. That's why I need you."

"Why don't I come over this afternoon to your office. But I'll need to talk to my partner first."

"Okay. How about 2:30?"

I agreed. I called Kelley but she didn't answer, so I called the office.

"Hello, Mr. Larson," Tina responded. "Yes, she's with a client, but I'll give her the message as soon as she's done."

Teddy came in the front door as I was fixing a little snack.

"Hey, Dad! How are you doing?"

"I'm not really sure, Son. How about you? Want a snack?"

"No. Charlie is stressed about her parents and school and college. I'm stressed for Charlie. What's going on with her folks anyway?"

"Well, Charlie's father was gambling again. Sometimes people with addictions backslide. Charlie's mother is trying to figure out the right thing to do. There is a lot of stress there."

"That makes sense."

"I suggested to Kelley that she stay at her mom's tonight to think about things. She's going to need her kids there, so you may need to give Charlie a break tonight."

"No problem. Okay if I hang out here with you this evening?"

I laughed. "Of course. You want to catch a ballgame? We could go see the Royals. I think they're playing the Yankees tonight."

"Sounds good. I'll text Charlie that you and I are doing something this evening. I have a couple things to do, so catch you about 6:00?"

"No later than 6:00, okay?"

Teddy nodded.

Kelley called. "Hey, Buck! I just have a minute. What's up?"

"Already have another case. Guy accused of murder over in Kansas City. His attorney called and I'm heading over to his office this afternoon."

"I loved working the last case. Are you okay if I say you do the leg work and I'll go back to more of a consultant role?"

"Under the circumstances, I'd say that's advisable. You know I don't mind."

"Thanks, Buck. I will be out at my mom's house tonight."

"I'm taking Teddy to a Royals game. That should give you some time with both Patrick and Charlie."

"You're a dear. I will talk to you later. I've got to go."

I got the Duo-Glide back out and headed over to Kansas City. Sometimes I got a little nervous about the Duo-Glide when I had to drive through in-town areas of Kansas City, but I needed the relaxation of the ride to get there. Ruby's office was down by the Country Club Plaza. I got off I-70 onto Seventh Street and eventually cut over to Ward Parkway as I got to the Missouri side of Kansas City. Turns off of Ward Parkway can be confusing which is bad for motorcycles especially since drivers often make erratic and sudden turns. Fortunately, there were no incidents in route.

I pulled into one of the many parking garages in the Plaza area and then headed over to Ruby's office. His office was on the second floor of one of the Plaza's outer buildings on up the hill. His secretary looked at me and smiled when I opened the door.

"You must be Buck Larson."

"If I must, then I am," I quipped.

The lady laughed. "You're quite the card. Just a minute. I'll let Mr. Ruby know you are here."

I looked around. There were filing cabinets randomly along the walls. It gave the impression of a long-standing law firm. Plants were scattered across the tops of some of the cabinets.

"Yes, I haven't redecorated in quite a while." Mr. Ruby came out and noticed I was looking about. "Mr. Larson, thank you for coming over."

"No problem, Mr. Ruby."

"Call me Andy. Let's go into my office."

We headed back to a corner office with stacks of papers piled up everywhere. I sat in a chair in front of his desk as he went around to his own desk chair. He pulled out a cigar.

"Care for a Cuban, Mr. Larson?"

"No, thanks. I don't smoke."

"Nasty habit! But I can't seem to quit." He chewed on an unlit cigar as we talked. "My client swears he didn't kill the girl. I guess almost all of them swear they didn't do it even if they did."

"Self-preservation. Yes."

"I really think he's telling the truth, Mr. Larson."

"Andy, call me Buck. So what's the scoop? What's the evidence against him?"

"The gun that killed her was his gun. At least, he admits purchasing it. He says he got it for her."

"What kind of gun?"

"An automatic that would fit into her purse. It's a .22"

"Easy to conceal, but lacking real knock-down power."

"True. And fingerprints, but on the barrel. The rest of it was wiped clean."

"Anything else?"

"Some love bird messages. Some saying he was absolutely done with her."

"Interesting. How long had he been in a relationship with the girl?"

"He says it was about 4 months. He says she was bonkers, and he ended it with her about 2 months ago, but she kept contacting him. Prosecutor is claiming that she wanted to end it and he wouldn't let go. Some of the messages, text and e-mail are confusing. Easy to construe one way or another."

"Okay, Andy. We'll take the case. When can I talk to your client?"

"I'll make arrangements for you to meet with him at the jail where he's being held. We haven't been able to get bond yet. Not sure we will be able to afford bond anyway. District Attorney would ask for it to be pretty high. Client says he is okay with just going straight to trial. The official plea was yesterday morning."

"I'm assuming he pled Not Guilty."

"He did. I prepared a file for you to get you started. Agnes has it on her desk. Thank you, again."

Agnes had the file ready. "I'm sure glad you're taking the case, Mr. Larson. I think the boy needs you on his team."

"Thanks, Agnes. I'll do my best."

I realized I was heading home just to head back to Kansas City. Teddy has his Plymouth and it would be good to let him drive. He loved that old red Valiant with the push-button gears.

I got back to the house before Teddy. I have to admit. I'm looking forward to some ballgame time with my son. It's been quite a while. We'd get some hot dogs and sodas at the game despite the price. I threw on a Royals shirt and ball cap just before I heard Teddy come in.

"Hey, Dad! Ready to go?"

"Yep. You want to drive? I'll cover the gas."

"Sure. Let me grab my Royals hat."

Teddy had a Royals hat that was more like a fishing hat. It had the circular brim and the vent holes along the side. We got it as a promo during one of the games a few years ago and it had become his lucky Royals hat.

Teddy headed down K-10 until we got to I-435 in Kansas City and then stayed on it on up to the stadium. Kauffman Stadium's lights were already on and with the Yankees playing, the crowd was a bit bigger. We ended up parking a little farther out, closer to Arrowhead Stadium which shares the parking lot. On those rare days when both the Chiefs and the Royals played, the parking lot was a mess.

I got a couple of Club Level tickets along the third base side of the stadium. While there was plenty of variety in food being sold, we stayed with the ballpark favorites of hotdogs and colas. I added a bag of peanuts. We found our seats and settled in as the players finished warm-ups.

"So, Dad, what do you think is going to happen between Charlie's folks?"

"I really don't know, Son. I don't think I could really guess."

"You really like Charlie's mom, don't you?"

I looked at Teddy. The truth was best. "I do, Son. But she's married and she knows that I don't want to influence her decisions about her marriage or be the reason she ends it."

"We know. It just makes us think."

"We? Us?"

"Charlie mentioned how much her mom likes you and how much you like her mom. I noticed, too. Charlie thinks her mom would be happier with you."

"I don't think that should be a topic for you guys."

"Oh, she loves her dad very much. She just sees how unhappy they are together. And, come one, Dad; it is a little weird that Charlie and I are dating, and you and her mom are so attracted to each other. Of course, it's going to get discussed."

"I don't know that it's weird. In a lot of ways it makes sense. There's a lot of me in you, and there is a lot of Kelley in Charlotte. I can see why you two are attracted to each other."

"I guess. Charlie and I are pretty serious about each other. I think we've both settled on going to North Carolina for college."

"UNC is a good school. I sure don't see any problems with that."

"Mom will probably stay out in Wilmington year-round if we do."

"I sort of guessed she would. She wants to be near you."

"Are you okay with that?"

"Son, I only want what's best for you. Whether you are near or far, we are always going to be close. That's just the way it is. You're stuck with me."

Teddy smiled. "Thanks, Dad. I love you."

"Love you, too, Son."

The game started and the Royals pitcher gave up an opening single before striking out the next batter. The third Yankee hit into a neat little double-play and the pitcher was out of the inning with 9 pitches. I had finished my hotdog and Teddy was almost done with his.

The Royals lead-off batter walked and stole a base on the first pitch to the second batter. The next pitch went flying deep into right field, but the Yankee outfielder was able to snag it while running toward the wall. There was one out with a runner on third. The next batter struck out, but the clean-up hitter ripped one into the fountain putting the Royals up 2-0. The fifth batter walked, but was thrown out trying to steal second. It looked like the Royals were going to play an aggressive game.

"Hot dogs! Get your hot dogs!" shouted a vendor walking up and down the aisles. I looked at Teddy and he nodded. We each had a second hot dog.

The score remained 2-0 through the 6th inning. In the top of the 7th, the Yankees centerfielder hit a towering shot into left field that landed on the pavilion. The Royals' starting pitcher was starting to struggle, but got the next two batters to fly out. With two outs, the Yankees' first baseman hit a shot into right field that barely cleared the wall. But it had, and the Yankees had tied the game. The next pitch brought a liner back at the pitcher who miraculously knocked it down and tossed it to first for the final out.

After singing Take Me Out to the Ballgame with the entire crowd, I opened the bag of peanuts. I usually saved them for the 7th inning stretch for luck. Unfortunately, the Royals went down in order.

The eighth inning went scoreless, but the top of the ninth saw the Yankees notch one more run to put them ahead. The Royals had the top of their line-up coming up in the ninth. The first batter hit a screaming liner down the third base line and just over the glove of the Yankee fielder. He pushed it to second for a double. The next batter laid down a perfect sacrifice bunt moving the runner to third. With one out and runner ready at third, the next batter took a big cut at the first pitch. It one-hopped to the shortstop who whizzed the ball to first after checking the runner back to third. Two outs. The clean-up hitter smacked a single into right field allowing the runner to score. It was 3-3 with two outs. The Royals inserted a pinch runner and the fifth batter bounced one past the pitcher and into center. The Royals had runners at the corners with two outs. The excitement was building in the stadium.

The runner at third managed a big lead and suddenly darted for the plate. The Yankee pitcher was so surprised, he dropped the ball and by the time he picked it up to throw home, the Royals had scored, taking the game 4-3.

We left the stadium with everyone cheering and talking about the last play. For Royals' fans, it was always good beating the New York Yankees. I imagined that was true in most major league parks other than Yankee Stadium, especially in the American League.

As we got into the car, I saw I had a text from Kelley. She asked me to call when I got the chance and hoped that the ballgame had been a fun one. I texted back that I was still with Teddy so I'd call once I got home if that was okay. She replied with an emoji smiley face.

When we got into town I had Teddy stop at Casey's so we could fill up his car. We were getting tired, but better to take care of things when you can. It was only a couple more blocks to our house.

Teddy opened the garage but I had to get out and move my Harley. I had left it close to the door. When I had finished moving the Duo-Glide, Teddy pulled his car on in and closed the door. We both headed upstairs into the house, tired and ready to get some sleep.

"Don't stay on the phone too long with Charlie, Son."

Teddy laughed. "Don't stay on the phone too long with Kelley, Dad."

I smiled. Like father, like son.

I called Kelley to see what was up. She sounded a little tired herself.

"How was the ballgame, Buck?"

"Exciting. Royals pulled out a squeaker. How are you doing?"

"I'm kind of numb at the moment. Victor and I have agreed to a trial separation. I'm going to see my attorney tomorrow to get the paperwork done."

"Is there anything I can do?"

"Victor is going to move out into an apartment for now. I don't think I'm going to be much help on the cases while this is going on, but I'll do what I can, when needed."

"It's okay. Do what you have to do."

"I talked to Charlie. She and Teddy are pretty serious."

"I know. I think they've settled on going to North Carolina."

"That's what she said. She also made an interesting observation."

"Is it that you'd be happier with me?"

"Yes. That was part of it. How did you know?"

"I just had a similar conversation with Teddy. Like I've said before, you know how I feel about you, but I can't be the reason for your break-up. I'll be there for you no matter what, but I shouldn't be the cause. And our kids. Well, I told Teddy there is a lot of me in him and a lot of you in Charlie."

"I know. You're not the cause, by the way. It was just interesting to hear one's own daughter suggest that you might be happier with someone else. And that the someone else be her boyfriend's father."

"That doesn't mean she doesn't love her dad. It's just her observation."

"That's true. I just wanted to let you know what was going on. I'm exhausted. I need to get some sleep."

"Do that. Take care, Kelley. I'm here if you need me."

"Thanks, Buck. You, too."

Chapter 13: Love Will Find a Way

There was a note on the kitchen table when I went downstairs for my coffee. Teddy let me know that he and Charlie were heading to the gym in Lawrence to work out and then would grab lunch. I fixed my coffee and sat down at the kitchen table. There was a lot to think about.

Kelley was becoming legally separated. I was very much in love with her. Her daughter and my son were dating. They were serious enough that they planned to go off to college in North Carolina together. They hadn't talked about living together, but I wouldn't be surprised if that came up soon. Charlie had already talked to her mom about the possibility of sex between them while in college.

The Morelli and Larson Detective Agency was established so that I would get a set pay for my detective work and a chance for Kelley and I to work together since, at the time, we couldn't be in a romantic relationship. That had now changed or at least seemed to have changed. Thinking of the agency reminded me that I did have a case and an appointment to meet with my client at the jailhouse.

I finished my coffee and headed up to take a quick shower. The phone rang as I got out to dry off.

"Good morning, Buck. I'm about to head to my attorney's. I was so tired, I forgot to ask you about the new case."

"I'm heading over in just a bit to talk to our client at the jailhouse. Mr. Ruby, Andy, is convinced Harold is innocent. Of course, he is his attorney. I'm pretty sure he truly does believe he's innocent."

"Let me know if you need me to do anything. Okay if I stop by this evening?"

"Let's have supper here together. Is that okay?"

"I'd like that. See you this evening."

The whole conversation had put me into a better mood. I got dressed and went down to the garage to get on the Duo-Glide. The bike fired up and sounded good. I was sure rolling up to a jail on a '58 Harley-Davidson Duo-Glide would make an impression. I hoped it would be the right one.

I arrived at the city jail and was let in. Andy had pre-arranged the interview with Harold, so once through the security check and signing in I got to meet with Harold Bowsman.

Harold was in his early 30s. He was about 5'10" tall and had an actor's look about him. Good looking guy with a photographic build, but you could tell he was soft. He didn't have the definition of action film actors. I could imagine that girls loved his looks. He had the wavy hair and blue eyes. He kind of looked like a young Elvis Presley but with lighter hair.

He sat down and looked at me when brought out from his cell. "Mr. Ruby says you're an investigator looking into my case."

"I am. Name's Buck Larson. I need to ask you a little about what happened with this girl, Patty, if I'm going to help."

"Patty Downset. Of course. What do you need to know?"

"How did you get to know, Patty?"

"She joined the Community Theater group I act with. We ended up in a one weekend play. One of the one's that they use as fillers between their big performances. It was a play by a local writer about two random people meeting and falling in love. It was really a very predictable play, but some like those quirky, romantic skits."

"You hadn't met her before that?"

"No. But we started going out after that. We got close really fast. Too fast. The relationship went from nothing to almost living together in days."

"Did you two talk about marriage?"

"In general. You know. One day it would be nice to have kids. I always pictured myself living in the country when I got married. I never proposed."

"But, you two were sleeping together? Living together?"

"We slept at one or the other's place most nights for a long while. She suggested moving in together to save money. I said it was better that we had our own places to retreat to if needed. One evening she had her parents over for dinner without telling me. Her parents were clearly under the impression we were engaged. I didn't want to embarrass her, but after they left I let her know I hadn't proposed. That marriage was not a given."

"How'd she take that?"

"It was weird. It was like she heard me, but acted as if I was kidding. She asked when she was going to meet my parents. I told her I wasn't going to be pushed into anything."

"Did you end it with her then?"

"No. She would show up at my place and we would talk and then we would end up in bed together. I know it was mixed messages, but I stopped going to her place and staying the night. She would constantly show up wherever I went. I think she must have bugged or put a location tracer on my phone. Eventually, I got a new phone."

"What did your friends think of Patty?"

"At first they liked her. Then it just seemed to be me and Patty doing things and my friends kind of stayed away. They thought it was just that girlfriend focus thing."

"So how long did you date Patty?"

"We were together for about 4 months. I finally told her 2 months or so ago that I wasn't gcing to see her anymore. Changed my lcck."

"Okay, tell me abcut the gun."

"She called right after we broke up and said she heard someone rattling her door. She said at first she thought it was me, but she fortunately looked through the keyhole before opening the door and saw a stranger. She said the guy noticed she was looking through the keyhole and, instead of running, smiled at her and banged the door hard. That scared her so she asked me to buy a gun for her that she could keep in the house."

"What did you get her?"

"I went over to a pawn shop and got her a cheap .22 automatic. I figured she's feel secure and it would be light enough for her to handle."

"How did your fingerprints get on the barrel?"

"She pointed it at me one time. She called saying the guy came back and wanted me to come over. When I went in, she pointed it at me, but said she wasn't even sure how to use it. I grabbed it since it was pointed at me and laid it down. I pointed out the trigger, the clip and explained how to use it. I suggested she find a pistol range and practice even."

"What about these texts?"

"I saw the texts. They are out of context. I try to be nice, Mr. Larson. I saw some of them. I did write how great she was. I was trying to make her feel okay. I get that some of them make it look like I was pursuing her, but those are edited and selective texts."

"And you deleted your own texts to and from her?"

"Of course."

"Tell me about her. What were her hobbies and interests?"

"She was a bit of a health food nut. She practiced yoga and self-meditation type things. She was a little bit of a hippie-type. I try to be careful with my food and exercise moderately, but she was into all of that. And she loved theater and drama. Kind of artsy."

"What about her friends?"

"I never met any of her friends and she didn't talk about any?"

"Do you know where she grew up? Where her hometown was?"

"She told me up in Michigan. Her parents flew down from Detroit, but I don't know that they necessarily live in Detroit."

"Where was she …, well, where did she die?"

"In her own place. In the tub."

"I may need to ask you some more questions later."

"I don't seem to be going anywhere, Mr. Larson."

I nodded and headed out. I'd need to see the crime scene. I called Mr. Ruby and he arranged for the two of us to visit the girl's apartment. An officer met us there to let us in and observe.

"So, what did you think of Mr. Bowsman?"

"I think he's too nice a guy. Or maybe too soft."

"What do you mean?"

"I think if he had been a bit more callous and not helped the lady after he broke up with her, a lot of this would have been avoided. He doesn't seem like he could have murdered her."

"But the evidence?"

"Explainable. A jury might think reasonable doubt."

"They might. Or they might feel it is enough to convict. There is a dead girl there and juries tend to think someone should pay the price for that."

"True, Andy. So, who else might want to kill her?"

We looked in the bathroom where Patty Downset had been shot. One shot, into the head, from just beyond arm's length away. There was a bullet hole in the tilework behind where Miss Downset's head would have rested. I placed a pen in the hole to look at the trajectory. It was from the other end of the tub.

"I need to look at the crime scene photos again. How tall was Miss Downset anyway?"

"Tallish. About 5'7" I believe."

"I don't think I need to see anything else. Where was the gun found?"

"It was in the tub. It is believed the shooter dropped it and didn't bother to recover it because of the noise of the shot. Or maybe they thought the fingerprints would dissolve in the soapy water."

Mr. Ruby let the police officer know we were done. We all headed out.

"Tell me, Buck. Are you getting anything that will help?"

"Definitely. When is the trial?"

"Starts next week."

"Good. I'm going to check on a couple more things and provide you with a report. I suspect you'll be putting me on the stand."

"Excellent. Do you think we can meet in a couple days to prepare?"

"Yes. I'm pretty sure that will work."

Andy Ruby returned to his office and I started to head back home. I looked at the file quickly and decided to go by the Yoga Center that Patty went to. It wasn't far away. Fortunately, it was open.

Inside there was a Yoga session going on. I talked quietly to a young lady at front desk. She knew Patty and said that her Yogi was the person leading the class in session. I asked her if I could wait. She smiled and pointed to an area where you could sit out of the way on a mat on the floor.

The middle-aged man leading the Yoga exercises walked over to the receptionist and then looked at me.

"Namaste. Can I be of some assistance?"

"I hope so. Do you remember Patty Downset?"

"Of course. Tragic what happened to her."

"Was she a regular here at your center?"

"She certainly was. At first, she came in once a week, but the last month before she … well, passed on, she was in at least 3 times a week."

"Was there a reason?"

"She said she had a boyfriend that wouldn't leave her alone. It was interesting, because for months before she had indicated she was rather in love with him. Young love! It changes."

"Was she working on anything special with all the sessions?"

"Funny you should ask. She was very much interested in flexibility and dexterity, even to the point of using individual toes for things."

"That is interesting. Are there exercises for that?"

"I had to develop some. Flexibility is built into the routine, but strengthening individual toes, that is different."

"How was her disposition?"

"She was always happy. Sometimes she would laugh during our meditation time. I had to remind her that others were focusing."

"Do you get many men in to do exercises?"

"Not many, but some. Are you interested?"

"I could sure use a little work on my flexibility. I might be."

"Well, we have general sessions set up about 5 times a day, Monday through Friday. That helps keep groups to no more than 10. Some are as small as 3. And we have weekend workshops."

"Did she make any friends here at the Yoga Center?"

"I never really saw her talking to anyone else much. She came, did her sessions, and left."

"Thank you. You've been helpful."

Stepping outside, I called Andy Ruby. "Andy, can you get a subsequent lab report on the body of Patty Downset?"

"Maybe. What for?"

"Can you do a whole-body check for powder burns? Head to toe?"

"What for?"

"I have a theory that may help."

"I'll get it started."

"Why don't I come back over to your office tomorrow? I've already got quite a bit."

"Sounds good. How about 11:00?"

"I'll be there."

I hopped on the Harley and decided I could take a round about way back home. I headed north and into Parkville. It's a pretty little town by the river. Park University is there commanding one of the hills. I took US 45 on up and cut over to Leavenworth before heading south again. The ride helped me clear my head and let me separate my thoughts about the case by the time I got back to Eudora.

Teddy texted saying he was going to be at his mom's this evening with Charlie. I gathered he wanted his mom and Charlie to get to know each other better.

I started getting some food ready for dinner. I planned on cooking a couple T-Bone steaks, making mashed potatoes, a little gravy, and green beans. I cut up some tomatoes and sliced mozzarella which I would drizzle with a special olive oil dressing. I had a nice wine picked out and ready.

With the food ready to be cooked and prepped, I looked at the file again. The more I looked at it, the case against Harold Bowsman seemed pretty thin. What had appeared on the surface as open and shut had a lot of little holes in it.

I was reviewing the file in the front room when Kelley knocked at the door. I opened the door to let her in.

"What are you working on?"

I hugged her and she smiled. I closed the file and handed it to her. "It's that murder case."

She opened it and scanned the reports. "What do you think?"

"I think I learned something from you on the last case that may bear fruit in this one."

"No pun intended?" I laughed having forgotten that what was missing in the last case was fruit. Cherries and peaches.

"Nope. But that's a good one."

"So what's missing?"

"A lot, but specifically powder burns."

"Interesting."

"Let's not look at the case right now. I have an appointment with the accused's attorney tomorrow. We are going to go over my theory and make preparation for court testimony."

"So, what should we do then?"

"I've got a wonderful dinner planned."

"Good. I'm starving."

The grill was hot. I reheated the mashed potatoes and made a little gravy on the stove while I got the steaks on the grill. I opened the wine and Kelley poured out the glasses and helped set the table. She had out the tomato and mozzarella beside our plates and I drizzled the olive oil mixture over them.

"Guess I forgot dinner rolls."

"It's okay, Buck. There are enough carbs here and it all looks delicious."

I plated the steaks and we sat down to enjoy a nice dinner.

"How was your day?"

"You want to know how it went with the attorney?"

"Yes. But also your day in general. You seem relaxed."

"I feel relaxed. The agreement was made for the legal separation. I will stay in the house. The kids will be with me, although there will be liberal visitation by the kids to their father. Patrick is actually staying at his dad's apartment this evening."

"Well, and Charlie is with Teddy at his mom's. He is staying out there tonight."

"Charlie is going to stay at my mom's again. They are doing some kind of project. Anyway, Victor and I will meet at the attorney's office once every two weeks to address the separation and what direction we will go. He's responsible for his own expenses and I'm responsible for mine, including the house. Neither of us has liability for or claim on the other's assets. I know you were worried about that."

"Sounds like it's amicable, so far."

"Yes. I think he and I both need to decide what we want. The kids seem okay about it so far."

We finished dinner and took our wine upstairs to the den. I put on some music to listen to as we chatted and unwound.

"I'm sorry I haven't been working this case with you. I enjoyed the last one."

"Kelley, you have enough to worry about. How did work go?"

"Oh, the usual. Anxieties. Relationship issues. Insecurities. My life in other people."

I laughed. "You're a pretty special lady."

"Thanks. By the way, did you know Danae is engaged?"

I wasn't sure if I should admit to knowing or not. I tried to play it safe.

"Oh, when did she tell you?"

"Today. She told me she had only confided in you so far, but only because of the state I was in."

"She seems happy."

"She does. James is planning on taking her up to the Wisconsin Dells toward the end of summer."

"That should be fun."

Kelley stretched out on the sofa. I pulled her shoes off and started rubbing her feet, massaging them.

"Oh, that feels good, Buck."

I smiled and she sipped a little more wine. There was a Neil Diamond song playing. Kelley started singing along quietly.

I sipped a little more wine and continued rubbing her feet.

"Buck," Kelley said rather dreamily, "I'm a little disappointed."

"Oh, was dinner not as good as you hoped?"

"Dinner was fine."

"Is the wine not to your taste?"

"The wine is wonderful."

"So, what is disappointing?"

"You haven't even tried to kiss me yet."

"I thought gentle touches and rubbing your feet might be in order first."

She sat up. "They are nice, but …"

I kissed her. Then I took her wine glass and set it aside with mine. I kissed her again, holding her to me. She laid back on the couch and I kissed her neck, biting playfully at her ear. I kissed her lips gently and then gave a tugging little bite to her lower lip. She returned the kisses. Passionate. Strong.

I began kissing below her neck and down her front. Her hands came up on my head and held me there. My arms were around her holding her. She moved her arms so they were around my neck and I picked her up, carrying her into my bedroom where I laid her gently on my bed.

Lying beside her I kissed her neck and lips again as I unbuttoned her top and got it from out around her. She wore a lacy, purple bra and her nipples were full pressing against the fabric. I continued kissing her while my hands explored the perfect rounded mounds on her chest. My fingers firmly squeezed her nipples and rubbed her, making her nipples even harder.

I relieved her of the bra and began kissing her breasts, sucking on her stiff nipples. I was touching her all over. Feeling her face, her neck. Running my hands across her skin. Kissing her body.

I lifted up and slide her slacks off her. Her matching, lacy purple panties were all that remained on her. She lifted my shirt off me and unzipped my pants. I wriggled out of the jeans and continued kissing her all over her body. My kisses on her belly-button brought about a cute, little giggle.

She was getting wet with anticipation as I became harder at the thought. I moved up, kissing her neck and face again as my hands massaged her breasts. She could feel my stiffness as it pushed against her panties. The lacy material barely holding me back.

I felt her heavy breathing and her kisses on my chest. I moved again, sliding her panties off her and admiring for a moment the beautiful body beneath me. The desire, the want had been there a long time. I lay down on top of her and teased at entering her. She became wetter and pushed her body up towards mine seeking satisfaction.

I gently slipped into her. The feeling was fantastic. I heard her moan. We began moving together. Thrusts building as I pushed hard into her, feeling her fingernails in my back pulling me to her. The sweat was building on our bodies, mixing with the wet buildup of making love. The movement powerful and the motion growing more rapid.

I held the final thrust as I released into her. She moaned out as almost a scream. Her legs squeezing me. Holding me there. I continued throbbing which added to the intensity. To make love to the one you most love is an unearthly pleasure.

When her legs relaxed, I moved beside her, still holding her and kissing her. She was shaking from it all. I pulled the covers over the two of us.

"Oh, my God, Buck! That was amazing!"

I was still breathing hard. I kissed her again and again.

"I love you, Kelley. You know I do."

"I do, Buck. Wow!"

We lay there looking at each. Touching each other gently. I ran my finger down her nose and smiled.

"Everything about you is beautiful."

She hugged me. "You know, I even brought over my purple silk pajamas that drove you crazy. I guess I didn't need them."

"You are sexy all by yourself."

"You're a sweetheart."

The music was still playing. Now it was a Barry Manilow tune. I got up and brought our wine into the bedroom. We finished off our glasses.

"This is nice, Buck."

"This is wonderful, Kelley."

She looked at me and nodded. I set the now empty wine glasses on the bedside table and kissed her again. Kissing her neck, her lips. I began touching her naked body again. She kissed me back, touching me. Her nipples started becoming hard again. I was getting hard again.

I moved on top of her, but then she rolled me back and got on top of me. My hands caressed her bottom as she guided me into her. She started moving up and down on top of me getting a rhythm as I moved up and into her. I watched her arch her back as we developed a concerted movement and I rubbed her breasts, squeezing and catching her nipples between my fingers. Her hands came down on my chest as we moved faster and faster. When I exploded into her again, her legs squeezed almost keeping me from moving. The throbbing continued and she dropped down, her chest against my chest. We lay there together, not moving, but with me still in her. It was a while before she rolled off me, moving her hair out of her face, allowing me to kiss her again and again.

"Darling," she said, "I have never felt so wonderfully spent."

She moved so that she was lying down beside me now, her back to me with my arms around her. Her arms held my arms to her.

"Goodnight, Sweetheart." I kissed the back of her neck.

"Goodnight," she happily mumbled. I could hear her deep breathing of sleep within a few minutes. I watched her as she slept. Never had I loved someone so much.

Chapter 14: Love Story

I woke up and found that I didn't just have a wonderful dream. There, sleeping beside me, was Kelley. Her hair was messed up, but she slept with a big smile. She looked happy.

I should have let her sleep, but I didn't. I ran my hands across her still naked body; my fingers gently gliding across sensitive areas. Her body responded as she slowly woke, getting wet again. She rolled over and I moved on top of her. She wrapped her legs around my legs.

I slowly entered her letting sensations build. Kelley hadn't opened her eyes, but she wore a smile as she stretched her arms and then wrapped them around me. My thrusts into her went from slow to faster and faster as our bodies began to take the stimulation to a new level. As the thrusts became stronger and faster, her eyes opened looking into mine. We looked at each other as our breathing became deeper and more rapid.

She felt the stream of fluid rush into her, pumping into her body. I saw her close her eyes with the pleasure.

"Morning sex is so good!"

I had to agree. It was wonderful being with her. We lay there a bit longer.

She looked at the clock. "I need to go home and get changed for work today." She kissed me on the cheek.

"I've got an appointment myself this morning."

She got up and pulled her clothes together in her arms. I kissed her and went downstairs to make coffee. She came down, dressed in her clothes from yesterday, just as I had both cups ready. We sat at the dining room table.

"I get a feeling I'm going to be smiling all day long, now." Kelley took another sip of coffee.

"I know I will. Makes it hard to focus on the case and the testimony. A pleasant distraction."

"I kind of feel like a teenager all-over again. Just kind of giddy."

I smiled. "I'm glad."

Kelley finished her coffee. "Buck, I have to go. I don't want to, but I have to."

I walked her to the door. She opened the door and I grabbed her and hugged her. She looked up at me and I kissed her. A long kiss. She grabbed my hand and then walked to her car waving before she got in.

I watched her drive off wondering when we would get the chance to be together again like that. Teddy had been out of the house, staying at his mom's. Charlie was at her grandmother's house for the night and Patrick spent the night with his dad. The stars had aligned for the moment.

I went up and showered. I dressed and made the bed. The sheets had gotten twisted and pulled out during the night and morning. I grabbed the wine glasses and took them downstairs to the kitchen putting them in the sink.

Grabbing the file off the table, I went down to the garage getting ready to head into Kansas City. I had plenty of time. The events of the evening played out in my mind as I guided the Duo-Glide toward Country Club Plaza and Andy's office.

Andy Ruby looked at me when I came into his office. "Are you okay?"

"Yea. Just had a good evening."

"Hmmm. You look like you're dream walking."

"Sorry. I do have a bit to go over with you." I shook myself out of the remembering of the night before and got down to business.

"Were you able to get the gun powder analysis done?"

"The prosecuting attorney objected. We can probably get the judge to order it. Not sure why she's fighting it."

"Probably because she's realizing her case is a lot weaker than it appears on the surface."

"I hope you're right. Let's hear your theory."

I started with the gun purchase. "I saw in the police report that the pawn shop owner said that Harold had told him that he was buying the gun for a girlfriend saying she was scared by an intruder."

"The prosecutor will say he was just planning out his alibi."

"But it also backs up his story. I think it will be a piece that solidifies his statement."

"Well, of course, the police have no record of the victim calling about a prowler."

"Let's look at the angle of the shot then."

"Shot right through her head."

"But the angle would have meant that the shooter practically had to be in the tub with her. It was a direct line from the other end of the tub. I don't see someone, especially someone 5'10" or taller, leaning over or bending down, hanging over the tub and shooting someone. It doesn't make sense."

"You've got a point, but then who shot her. Are you saying someone was in the tub with her?"

"Hardly. A person in the tub with her would hardly have dropped the gun into the tub. Besides, that dynamic just doesn't fit - slipping into a tub with a gun."

"So, who shot her?"

"She shot herself. That's why I want the gun powder testing."

"Wait! Her arms don't reach that far. It's a 6 foot tub."

"She had been planning this. Her yoga instructor shared that she had been working this last month or so on flexibility and toe strength."

"Toe strength?"

"Toe strength. It is an almost perfectly planned frame up of Harold."

"What? I don't get it."

"She was a tad bit nuts. She realized Harold wasn't going to marry her, so she plans out a suicide that will frame him for murder. If I'm right, there will be powder burns along her left toes and ankle where she held the gun with her feet. She used her right toe to pull the trigger. The gun, which she had managed to get Harold to buy for her and made sure his fingerprints were on, dropped into the water, appearing to be out of reach for her. She even had used the soap to write his initials on the tub tile. That, in itself, is interesting since the report indicated she died instantaneously from the gunshot to the head."

"It does start to become a flimsy case. Wow!"

"The case against him will all fall apart with the gunpowder residue report."

"And I suspect that's why the prosecuting attorney is fighting it."

"I assume you will want to depose the yogi. I have his name and business address in the file."

"I'll probably need you to testify, Buck. This is great."

"This is what you hired us for."

"How about lunch? I'm buying."

We went over to the Plaza proper and dined at Tomfooleries. It was a lunch I very much enjoyed. Other than coffee, I hadn't eaten anything since supper yesterday. After lunch, I checked with Andy about the trial. He indicated that the trial date was up quick, next week.

"Seems like another push by the prosecutor to rush things."

"I was about to file for a continuance, but I think this will surprise them. I suspect they thought they were going to have to argue about moving along so quickly. We'll not stop this going ahead. I'll also ask the judge to order the gunpowder test to be conducted."

"You've got my number." We headed back to Andy's office and I jumped on my bike as he went inside. I saw the double-take as I motorcycled away.

I was feeling good by the time I got back home. Life seemed to be going well. I called Kelley to see how she was doing.

"Hey, Buck. Good timing. I'm between clients. How did your meeting go?"

"Great. It will go to trial, but I'm confident our client will be found not guilty if they don't just dismiss the case altogether. How's your day gone?"

"I keep smiling. Tina kind of looked at me oddly, but she hasn't asked anything. Danae has been pretty busy between clients and thinking about her own wedding."

"What are you doing this evening?"

"The kids and I are having an evening at home. I'm sure they have a lot of questions and I need some time with just them."

"Understandable. I think Teddy has an astronomy class assignment that he's doing tonight. He wanted me to help him set up his telescope to observe some meteor shower tonight."

"Buck, I loved last night. And this morning."

"Me, too."

Kelley went back to her work and I decided that with the late night looking at stars coming up, a nap might be in order. I went upstairs and stretched out across the top of the bed. I could still smell Kelley's scent on the pillow she had laid her head on last night.

Teddy popped in around supper time. He offered to cook something, but I was in the mood for more than mac and cheese. I suggested we go up to Jasmin's, the local restaurant. He agreed readily making me think that might have been his plan in the first place.

It was a nice evening and we walked up the couple of blocks to the restaurant. Jasmin greeted us when we came in and grabbed us a couple of waters before taking our order. I was in the mood for chile rellenos and Teddy went with the burrito plate.

"Dad, do you still think we can head out to North Carolina for a college visit? Might be a little more awkward, but Charlie and I are still interested in attending UNC."

"Well, I don't think the current situation has changed that too much. The logistics might change a little for families, but the visit should still be a go."

"I wasn't sure. With Charlie's parents being separated. I didn't know how things would end up."

"It should have nothing to do with your plans. Charlie's may need to adjust a little, but I don't think much. And what you two decide together shouldn't have to be based on her parents' situation. Or even your parents' situation."

"I didn't know if it made it even more awkward for you. I mean, we can tell how close you are to Dr. Morgan."

"Regardless, it shouldn't impact what you two do."

"What if we decide to get a place together?"

"Wow! Son, that's a big step. Not one to take lightly. That's something a little beyond just you and Charlie, but it still shouldn't be impacted by what is going on with her parents."

"Actually, mom thought you'd probably be okay with it."

"Your mother is okay with that!"

“She said she was glad I discussed it with her and since, it is a year away, it is probably better to talk about it and think it over.”

“That’s very … um, progressive of your mom. You’ll both be 18 and, basically, you both appear to be going on scholarship. My point is, technically, you’ll both be independent adults. Young adults, but adults just the same. We’ve talked about the responsibilities of being an adult. Of being a trustworthy male.”

“I know, Dad.”

“So, what is your plan?”

“Like you said, we’ve both got scholarships that we can apply to going to UNC. We both want to go there together. I’ve got family out there should there be trouble. But, Dad, that’s only an emergency. You know I saved up quite a bit of money. Granted you and mom, well grandma and grandpa, have given me a lot, but I have saved it.”

“Yes, you have. I’m proud of your sense of responsibility with money.”

“Charlie and I have talked about getting a small house in Chapel Hill or at least close by. I know you think I only make food out of the box, but I’m learning. It won't be easy. If Charlie is on a basketball scholarship, then she'll have a big commitment. Honestly though, there are married men playing college basketball and football. There is as much required of them and less concern."

"Except the women's teams, whether fair or not, tend to frown on married players. It's a double standard, but it exists."

"Charlie knows that. Actually, one of the reasons we are holding off on getting married first is because of that."

"Well, I'm glad we're talking about it now. Ultimately the decision is yours and Charlie's. Your mom and I and Charlie's parents will certainly provide input, but it's your life. And, truly, I can't say that your wrong."

Our food arrived. I smiled and mussed up Teddy's hair. He reached up and fixed it with a laugh.

"You're the best, Dad."

"If you say so, Son."

We walked back to the house. It was still a couple hours before it would get anywhere near dark enough for watching the sky for astrological phenomena. Teddy said he was going to lie down for a little bit, but made me promise to check on him by 9:00 just in case he dozed off.

I went upstairs and sat down. About an hour later, I got a text from Kelley asking me to call if I could. I called.

"What's up, beautiful?"

"Aww. You're sweet. Charlie told me that she and Teddy are thinking about living together at college."

"Yep. Teddy has enough set aside to buy a small house. He talked to me at supper to see what I thought."

"Must have been a concerted effort by the two of them. That's when Charlie let me know. What did you say to him?"

"I told him that I was glad he was bringing it up now so we could talk about it and think about it. I let him know that ultimately it was his and Charlie's decision, but he should expect a lot of opinions offered."

"Buck, we … well, you know."

"You are limited in your talking at the moment is what you are trying to say."

"Yes. I guess hearing that, right now. Well, to me, she's still my baby. But you are right. The decision will be their own. It's just happening so fast."

"We've got two bright kids. And if we support them the best way possible, they'll be okay."

"Buck, this feels a little weird."

"Hey, be glad I don't have a daughter about Patrick's age."

"Oh God! That's mean." Kelley paused and laughed. "How was your dinner?"

"Nice. We went up to Jasmin's. Teddy is resting before our night sky watch."

"I don't think I could stay up after last night. Good luck with that."

"I took an afternoon nap in preparation. Your scent was still on the pillow."

"Buck!" Nothing was said for a moment before Kelley added, "I'm glad."

"We do need to plan a Carolina trip. We promised the kids."

"I know. I also need to coordinate with Danae. Remember James is taking her to the Wisconsin Dells. Didn't you say you'd have to testify in this latest case? When is the trial?"

"Next week."

"That's fast."

"Yes. The prosecuting attorney is trying to move quickly. I think there are a few facts that she hoped wouldn't be looked at."

"Enjoy your night excursion. I'm going to get back with the kids. We've been playing some card and board games while we chat. We are all in the middle of a snack break." I could hear the kids calling for their mom in the background.

The North Carolina trip was going to be a rather interesting adventure. I didn't know if Victor would go, but there was no reason to assume he wouldn't, particularly if he and Kelley were being amicable about things. Trudy's family was already out there about two hours away from Chapel Hill at the most. I started to wonder if I was needed out there. I guess I'd talk to Teddy about it, but I didn't want to give the impression that I didn't want to go. Trudy was out here in Kansas right now, but she'd definitely want to go back to North Carolina for that.

I looked at the clock and went down to make sure Teddy was awake. I knocked on his door.

"I'm awake, Dad. Thanks."

I got out the Jeep and packed Teddy's telescope into the back. We had gotten special permission to use Wells' Overlook south of Lawrence beyond the regular park time. We had explained about the meteor shower. A few amateur astronomers would be out at Clinton Lake on this clear night.

We headed on out with the windows down and cutting through the county roads over to the tower which rose above the big hill overlooking Lawrence. The city lights below were far enough away that they interfered little with the telescope pointing upward toward the cloudless skies.

It was close to 11:00 when the sky spectacular hit its early peak. Two, three, five meteors would light up the sky every few minutes. It was beautiful. Teddy took notes, made drawings, and even snapped pics through the telescope during the show. We stayed longer than we planned, finally wrapping things up around 1:00 a.m. when only a single meteor would appear in a ten-minute span. Still beautiful, but the earlier light show had been mesmerizing.

We got back home and I was yawning. "Don't spend too much time putting your preliminary report together tonight."

"Not too long, Dad. Thanks for going out with me."

"Hey, thanks for sharing that with me. Goodnight, Son."

"Goodnight, Dad."

I had just laid down when I got a text from Kelley. She let me know she was thinking of me. I texted back asking her how she knew I just got home. Her reply was that Teddy and Charlie were texting. I should have known.

Chapter 15: Love Means Zero

Andy called a couple days later to say the judge not only granted the gunpowder residue test, but had reprimanded Janice Alvarez, the prosecuting attorney for trying to block the acquisition of evidence. There might even be a reprimand from the Missouri Bar.

"That will help keep the questionable tactics down in the trial. I wouldn't think an attorney could afford too many reprimands."

"That's true, Buck. I was hoping she would drop the case, but the publicity she generated with it has put her in a spot. She's new and has some high aspirations politically. By the way, the lab results showed, just as you suggested, powder burns on her lower left leg and foot."

"With that, I would think that this should go well for Mr. Harold Bowsman."

"Jury selection is tomorrow, and we will start the trial on Monday unless she changes her mind and the charges are dropped. The prosecutor actually asked for a continuance. The judge denied it indicating she had pushed for an expedited trial and she was the one who delayed the gathering of evidence after that."

"The judge doesn't sound happy with her."

"Nope. Not at all."

I hung up the phone knowing that I would be in court during the next week. I called Kelley to see if she'd like to have lunch together. We agreed to meet over at Paisano's for Italian.

I got to Paisano's a little early and waited out front for Kelley. She pulled up and I could see her smile when she saw me. I walked over to open the door for her after she finished parking.

"Such a gentleman."

"I do try." I gave her a hug and we headed on in to eat.

I ordered pasta with Italian sausage and diablo sauce. Kelley ordered pasta carbonara. The salad and some breadsticks came out right away. The waiter asked us what we wanted to drink.

"Are you up for some wine?"

"I'm going to stick with water. I've still got clients coming in this afternoon and my stomach's been a little upset."

I went with iced tea since Kelley was having water. I think of wine as more of a social drink.

"Buck, what do you think of our kids possibly living together? I can't help but keep thinking about it."

"Are you warming to the idea?"

"I don't know if I would call it warming or just adjusting to it."

"I think they are being mature about it. I do worry that they're pretty young to be making that decision. On the other hand, many of their classmates will end up marrying right out of high school and not go to college."

"It's just a lot. Especially with everything going on."

The waiter brought out of lunch. We continued talking as we ate. I talked in general about the case. Kelley talked in generalities regarding her clients. As we got near the end of lunch, I noticed Kelley hadn't eaten much.

"Are you okay? You didn't eat much."

"I think all the stress is getting to me. Along with Charlie getting ready for college and her relationship with Teddy, I have my separation meeting again tomorrow with Victor."

"I was under the impression that things are going along amicably. Am I wrong?"

"No. No arguments. I do think I need to talk to him about Charlotte's plans. She was a little nervous about letting her father know."

"Well, you're being nice about that. You could point out that being an adult is taking responsibility and she should tell him."

"I don't think I can do that to her. I'll take care of it."

I had the waiter bring out a to-go box for the rest of Kelley's lunch. He boxed it up and put it in a bag for us. I walked Kelley out to her car. She held on to my arm as we walked.

"There is so much going on, Buck. So much is happening so quickly."

"I know. Way too fast."

She got into her Jaguar. "I'll call or text you later," she said before shutting her door.

I smiled and waved at her as she headed back to work. She waved and blew me a kiss as she was leaving.

I spent the afternoon just cruising around on the Harley doing one of my favorite things, heading out to anywhere and just letting the road take me for an afternoon ride. I managed to cut through the Flint Hills and then up toward Fort Riley, Home of the Big Red One. I cut through Manhattan and past Kansas State University before working my way back east toward home. Sometimes the road stretched out flat and straight. Other times it circled up hills and along rivers. It was a time to just let go. It was relaxing.

The next day, I popped by Kelley and Danae's office to give some billing items to Tina.

"Kelley is out, Mr. Larson," Tina informed me.

"I know. She has one of her separation meetings today." Tina looked relieved that I knew and she wasn't the one that told me.

"How is it going with Danny?"

"It's great. He is taking me to the Old Shawnee Days." Tina looked worried for a second. "I'm sorry. I didn't check with you to see that it's okay to take a day."

"Tina, if you clear it here, then it's okay."

"Thanks, Mr. Larson. I'm looking forward to the parade and the rides. I guess I'm just a little kid about those things."

"Nothing wrong with that. Enjoy."

Danae came out. "I thought I heard your voice. How's it going?"

"Almost too smoothly. It worries me when things go too smoothly. How are you doing?"

"Getting ready to go up to the Dells next week with James. I've not been before."

"You'll love it. Have you settled on a date for the wedding?"

"We're looking at the end of September. I'd like an outdoor wedding and it would be nice if it were comfortable."

"I agree. Should be plenty of places available for an outside ceremony."

"We are looking at a few. I'm excited. By the way, isn't your trial next week?"

"Well, not my trial. At least I hope not. But yes, I will be in court some next week."

"Good luck with that."

"Thanks. Tell Kelley I was by if you see her."

Danae went back into her office. I passed by a client coming in as I left. I noticed the client look back at me with that 'I've seen him somewhere before' look.

I spent a leisurely afternoon at home. It was almost supper when Kelley called.

"Hey there, Sexy!"

"Hi, Buck. Can I come by and talk with you for a bit?"

"Sure. Do you want me to fix supper?"

"No. I'm not really hungry. Just want to see you for a little while."

"I'm here and I don't have any plans."

"Okay. See you in a few."

I made sure the house was tidy and that I had cleaned up the dishes. For the most part, I keep everything neat anyway. I checked Teddy's room. It was very well kept, especially for a teenaged boy. He was 17 now and getting ready to head off to college after this coming year.

Kelley pulled up out front and knocked. I opened the door and gave her a hug. She hugged me back before we went up to the den.

"Do you want a drink?"

"Just some water. My stomach is still bothering me." She looked nervous.

I brought her a bottle of Perrier which I had opened for her. "Thanks. Maybe the bubbles will help." She laughed.

"What's the matter? Did your meeting go okay today?"

"Yes." She paused. "No." She paused again. "I don't know exactly how I'd characterize it right now."

I sat down beside her and took her hand. She pulled it back.

"I'm sorry, Buck. Victor and I talked. We are going to give it one more try."

That wasn't at all what I had expected. I looked at her kind of stunned. I suppose in the back of my mine I realized that a trial separation could go either way, end in dissolution of the marriage or it could result in a reconciliation. My own thoughts had already gone with the former and I was now being hit with the latter.

Kelley started to cry. "Say something, Buck. I'm not sure if you're upset with me or hate me or what? I don't know."

"Kelley." I took her hand and held it not letting her withdraw it from me. "When I couldn't have you, I loved you. For this brief time that I could have you, I loved you. Nothing has changed how I FEEL about you. You know I love you."

She began crying more. "I … I really thought that … Honestly, I don't know what I thought. Under the circumstances, I gave in to feelings I have for you that I couldn't act on. I still feel them."

"I understand that your situation is not easy. You have two children with Victor. You love him and you married him."

"But I … I also felt betrayed by him."

"Kelley - and I am not saying this to hurt you - but I think you feel like you betrayed him, too. I didn't realize that before. I probably didn't want to think it. You're looking to give him another chance. There's nothing wrong with that. You and I will be okay. Of course, I hurt. But it's because how I feel about you, not because I feel betrayed."

"Are you sure?"

"I'm sure. I'm your friend as well. That doesn't stop. Not now. I suspect now you're going to need me as a friend more than ever."

"I don't want to lose our friendship, but regardless, after this past week, it has changed."

"Somewhat. It's a precious moment in my life."

"Mine, too. I told Victor that we had gone on some dates. I didn't think he needed the details. I don't think he wants to know. I even told him I needed to come out her to talk to you in person."

"You're a good person, Dr. Morgan."

"Am I? I don't know."

"You are. Don't question it."

"Buck, we talked about moving to start over. With Charlie thinking about going to UNC, we discussed moving to North Carolina."

"This isn't to keep Charlie and Teddy from living together, is it?"

"No. I even said that if we move, it shouldn't be to Chapel Hill. He mentioned Wilmington ironically."

"Close to the ocean. It's nice there."

"No decision yet. There's a lot to decide and do. I do think I should end my business partnership with the detective agency. At least as an active partner."

"I can buy out your half if you like. Well, if you feel it's needed."

"I didn't invest anything."

"Okay, let's just split the profits from the cases we've taken so far."

"The first two."

"The one I'm on now, too. It will be the sole three cases of The Morelli and Larson Detective Agency. Maybe

I'll keep the name even though it will just be Larson."

"You're a special breed." She hugged me. "Thank you, Buck for being so understanding."

"That's me. Mr. Understanding."

"Don't make me cry again." She got up.

I walked her to the front door and then turned her. "You'll have to excuse me." I kissed her long and hard. And then I walked her on out to her car and opened her door. She looked up sadly. "Kelley, we are still friends. We will do lunch. We will flirt with each other knowing we can't follow through." She laughed and nodded. "It will be okay."

I watched her drive away. It was sad. I realized once again that I was doomed to be unlucky in love. It had been that way and it hadn't changed. It wasn't Kelley's fault; it was the life force that surrounded me. I was definitely going to have a drink this evening. Probably many.

The next day, Teddy came upstairs to check on me. I didn't realize how late I had slept in.

"Dad, are you feeling okay?"

I rolled over and looked at him. "Sure, Son. Why?"

"It's 9:00 in the morning. I don't think you've ever in my life slept in this late."

"Rough night sleeping. I'm getting up. Do you want breakfast?"

Teddy laughed. "I already had breakfast. I'm heading to the gym to workout with Charlie."

"Okay, Son. Let's plan on supper together tonight. Invite Charlie over if you want."

"I'll check with her, but sounds good."

I heard Teddy clomp down the stairs and get into his car. He headed off. Must be weekend I said to myself.

I didn't really have a hangover, but I probably drank a little more than usual the previous night. I looked at my phone. Kelley had texted earlier that she hoped I was okay and would have a good Saturday. It had come in about an hour and a half earlier. I debated texting back.

I realized the dilemma. I didn't want to interrupt yet didn't want to appear I was ignoring her. Damn I was over thinking this. I texted back that I slept in late and wished her a good weekend. With that, I went down to grab some coffee.

The sun was bright through the kitchen window. I made up my mind to take care of some things around the house. While sipping coffee, I made a mental list. Vacuum area rugs. Sweep and mop wood floors. Dust. Wow! How long had it been since I dusted? Mow yard. No. I hired a kid who mowed the yard. I knew it was good money for him and he trimmed the bushes and edged. The Jeep needed an oil change. I added it to my list. I realized I was setting up chores to keep me from thinking.

I threw on some old gym shorts and a t-shirt and started cleaning up. There was a call when I had finished mopping the upper level floors. It was Andy Ruby.

"Hope I'm not bothering you, Buck."

"No problem, Andy. What's up? When do you need me?"

"I got the judge to let you sit at the defense table with me. Can you be at court on Monday at 9:00?"

"Sure, but why?"

"You've got a good mind. You're smart. It would be good to have you at the table."

"You want numbers."

"See. I told you, you were smart."

"You're paying. It doesn't matter to me where I sit as long as it's not the electric chair."

"Good one. Don't use that in court."

"I'll see you Monday, Andy."

I finished up the mopping downstairs and had cleared the bathrooms. I was staring to run out of chores. The dusting hadn't taken as long as I thought it would and I did it after sweeping, but before mopping. Just the process my mom taught me.

There was a knock on the door. I saw Ed Hatfield, Chief of Police standing there.

"Come on in, Ed."

"You've been a bit of a stranger."

"Where's Erin?"

"Who do you think sent me to check on you?"

"Coffee?"

"Of course." We headed back to the kitchen. "What's going on?"

"Sit down. I'll provide you enough for your report back to your wife."

We had our coffees and stretched out. I started with the situation with Teddy and Charlie.

"You're being more open minded about this than I'd be. What does Charlie's mom think of it?"

"She's coming around to it. Not her preferred situation."

"And speaking of Charlie's mom, how's it going with her?"

I thought a moment before saying anything. "Victor went gambling again while Kelley and I were on the last case. They had a trial separation but are back together now giving it another try."

"Oh, Erin won't like that. She thinks you and Kelley should be together."

"Well, they may be moving to North Carolina for a fresh start and to be closer to Charlie when she does go to school."

"Makes sense. Where does that leave you?"

"What do you mean?"

"Thought you two were in this detective business together."

"Oh, that. She is dropping out, taking her share of the money from the cases we had prior to the partnership split."

"How are you doing then?"

"You know me."

"Yes, I know you. That's why I ask, because, darn it, you won't tell."

"I'm fine."

"How about dinner tonight?"

"Not tonight. I have Teddy and he's bringing over Charlie."

"Alright." Ed finished his coffee. "Stop being a stranger. We don't like it and Erin nags me about what you're up to when she doesn't hear for herself."

I picked up some plantains after getting the oil changed in the Jeep. At home, I prepared them to make tostones for the evening meal. I put some chicken and rice in a large pan, seasoning with saffron and some other Latin spices. As the arroz con pollo cooked, I put together a non-alcoholic creamy coconut concoction that would be refreshing and a balance against the spicy chicken and rice.

Charlie and Teddy walked in just as I getting the sliced plantain into the frying pan.

"Wow! Something smells good, Mr. Larson."

"Oh, Dad can cook. That's arroz con pollo and it looks like he's making tostones."

"I'm not sure what either is, Teddy."

"Um, chicken in rice and fried plantains. Plantains are like bananas."

I stood there with a couple of coconut coolers for the kids. They took them and took a sip.

"Yum!" Charlie declared.

The kids kept me company in the kitchen and as the food was ready, I dished up a plate for both of them and then myself. We all sat down at the kitchen table.

"So, Charlie, any updates on your plans?"

"Well, I think mom told you that they were thinking of moving to North Carolina. Mom says it would be a fresh start for dad and her. I think it's to keep an eye on me."

I laughed. "Probably a combination of the two."

"Anyway, it opens up some options. Teddy and I were talking that if they do move, and it's close enough, I might commute in and he could either stay in the dorm or get the house and live there."

Teddy finished his bite. "If I get the house regardless, I could sell it when we graduate and probably make a little profit."

I agreed. "You might just do that. I know some families that have bought houses and then rented rooms out to their kid's friends, making some money while there and a profit when they sold after they left."

"We haven't totally given up on the idea of living together either, Dad."

"I get it, keep your options open."

"Mr. Larson?" Charlie hesitantly asked. "Are you and my mom okay?"

"Yeah, I think so. Why?"

"Well, pardon my observation, but we can tell you have a thing for my mom. And she does for you. Frankly, I thought the two of you might end up together when my folks separated."

"Charlie, I'm fine. I very much care for your mom, but she and your dad need to see how things work out. She tells me she's fine and I have no reason to doubt her."

"I do." Charlie looked down and had another bite.

"I don't know what to tell you, Sweetheart. Life is rather complicated."

"I know. She just cries sometimes when she doesn't think anyone is around."

"Sometimes we have to let hurt out. Let her have her private moments.

Have you decided on a major? Are you still going to be a psychologist?"

"That's my plan. Maybe mom and I can work together one of these days."

"That's a beautiful plan. What about you, Son? Settled on a major?"

"Dad, I don't know that I've settled on one, but I'm looking at pre-Med."

"That's not something you've talked a lot about before. Pre-Law, but not Pre-Med."

"Pre-Law is Grandpa Ryan's idea. I don't mean to be rude, but that's his dream, not mine."

"I think you get wiser every day, Son."

We finished off the meal and cleaned up. The three of us were then just standing there, hanging in the kitchen.

"Son, were you two going to a movie or something?"

"Nope. We decided to spend time with you."

"Okay, let's go."

Teddy and Charlie looked at each other quizzically. Then they followed me out the front door. I stood by Teddy's car. "You have to drive, Son."

We all got in. I was a little cramped in the back seat, but I managed.

"Where to, Dad?"

"The Bowling Alley!"

"Seriously, Dad." Teddy laughed. "We haven't gone in years."

"It sounds like fun," Charlie said.

We hit the lanes in Lawrence. It was fun. Charlie, being a natural athlete, bowled a 132 despite not having bowled since she was a little kid. Teddy and I were vying for top honors. Teddy scored a 189. I finished out with a 200.

"One more game, Dad." We all agreed. Charlie got a 167. Teddy bowled a 202. It was not my best game. I scored a 165 behind both of the kids.

"That's it for me, kids. I don't think I could bowl another game tonight."

Charlie was hyped up. "That was fun. I need to get mom out bowling."

"I'm sure she would enjoy it, Charlie," I replied.

"I think you let me win that second game, Dad."

"Have I ever LET you win a game since you were 5?"

"No. I guess not."

I had Teddy drop me off at home first so that he and Charlie could have some private time. It was a Saturday evening. I had been home about a half-hour when I got a call from Kelley.

"Sounds like you had a good time with the kids."

"I did. I guess they told you."

"They did. Actually, they're still both here. I've been told I need to go bowling with them. You seemed to have started something."

"Maybe. It's a fun activity."

"Thanks for being so good about all this."

"That's what friends do."

"You really are a good friend. Sweet dreams."

"Goodnight, Kelley."

When Monday morning rolled around, I found myself doing something I don't like doing. I put on a tie. It was court and now I was to be sitting at the defense table. And there was going to be another thing. I would have to take the Jeep. It was summer and motorcycle weather. It would be a long week. I grabbed my files and headed out.

Teddy saw me and did a double take.

"Don't say a thing, Son. Not a thing."

He laughed and went to fix himself some breakfast. I saw him getting his phone out as I was leaving. No secrets in this house.

I got to court about 8:15, well enough early. I sat down at the defense table toward the end. At about 8:40, Andy appeared.

"They're suppose to have Harold here shortly." As he said that, the jailors escorted him to the table.

Mr. Ruby went over the case in brief with the accused, who mainly nodded. He explained that I would provide testimony on the results of the investigation and that the plan at the moment was to invoke his 5th Amendment right against testifying.

The prosecuting attorney came in and put some notes on the table. Then she did a double-take at our table.

The judge promptly entered the courtroom at 9:00. We rose and were seated. Judge Allison Nichols took her position very seriously as a servant of the people.

"Your honor," Janice Alvarez began, "I object to the additional person at the defense table."

"On what grounds?" Judge Nichols looked annoyed.

"I was given no notice of another attorney."

"First, Ms. Alvarez, Mr. Larson is not another attorney. Second, Mr. Ruby petitioned the court for his inclusion which your office was provided notice of by this court and did not make an objection before I granted the request."

"I did not receive the notice. It seems highly irregular."

"Council will approach." Ms. Alvarez and Mr. Ruby walked up to the judge's bench. There was a very short discussion and the attorney's returned to their tables. Ruby had a smile on his face.

Andy leaned over and whispered that the Judge was already not happy with the prosecutor and would tolerate no more courtroom show.

Judge Nichols looked over at the Defense Table. "Mr. Larson, you understand that you are not a lawyer. You may provide information to Mr. Ryan at the table and, if called, you may testify in accordance with the rules for witnesses. Do you understand?"

I stood up. "Yes, you honor."

"You may sit back down." The judge looked at Ms. Alvarez. "Unless there are any valid preliminary motions, you may begin with your opening statement."

Ms. Alvarez got up. "Thank you, your honor." She walked over to the jury. "We will show that the accused, Mr. Bowsman, purchase a gun and then went to Miss Downset's apartment, shooting and killing her. There will be no question that he purchased the gun. We will show that the two individuals dated for some time and when Miss Downset ended the relationship, he became upset and tried to win her back. When that failed, he went to her apartment, where he had been many times before and killed her. The victim, in her dying moments, used soap to write his initials on the tile around the tub, identifying her assailant."

She turned dramatically to look at Harold. She pointed at him. "He took a life so young, because she rejected him. Now, we just want justice for her."

With that the prosecutor sat down. The jury looked hard at Harold Bowsman. They looked ready to find him guilty then and there.

The judge looked over at Andy. "Your opening remarks, Mr. Ruby."

Andy got up and stood in front of the table. "Thank you, Your Honor. Ladies and Gentlemen of the Jury, this case was poorly investigated and is poorly thought out. We will show that Mr. Bowsman not only couldn't have committed this murder, we will show who actually did conduct this crime. We will not argue the fact that Mr. Bowsman purchased the gun. He did so and didn't try to hide the fact. He did so at the request of the victim herself. There is not question that the two dated, but what was construed as Miss Downset ending the relationship is actually Mr. Bowsman ending the relationship. Unfortunately, rather than following the facts in this case, the prosecution turned the facts to try to fit their theory. We will show emphatically that the facts do not."

Andy moved toward the prosecution table. "In fact, the evidence that shows this was suppressed by the prosecutor herself."

"Objection!" shouted the prosecutor.

"Sustained," the judge ruled. "Mr. Boyd, you had your motion for evidence obtainment granted by the court. Do not suggest motive by the prosecutor for arguing against the motion."

Andy had put it out there for the jury to see that the prosecutor had tried not to play fair. He continued. "My apologies, Your Honor. With the evidence, Ladies and Gentlemen, we will show that another person fired that gun. We will show from the forensics that it would be all but impossible for my client to have shot her. The rush for trial in the case seems to be a rush for judgment. Thank you."

"Objection!"

"On what grounds, Ms. Alvarez?"

"The defense is making it appear that we didn't do a full investigation."

"Approach, Ms. Alvarez."

Mr. Ruby got up but the judge put up her hand to halt him. There was some type of reprimand and the prosecutor returned to her seat fuming.

The prosecution called witnesses. First the pawn shop owner who sold he gun. He identified Harold as the person who purchased the gun and had specifically asked for that type of gun.

On cross examination, Andy asked him what was said about why he bought the gun. The pawn shop owner told him that he had said his girlfriend was scared and asked him to buy it for her.

"Did he seem sincere in telling you that?"

"Yes, I believed him."

On redirect, the prosecutor only had one question. "Are you sure he used the term 'girlfriend,' Sir?"

"Yes. I'm pretty sure that was what he said."

The next witness was the police officer who arrived at the scene. He indicated that a neighbor had called because he heard a loud bang that sounded like a gun shot but he wasn't sure. The officer arrived and when no one answered, had the apartment superintendent unlocked the door. He walked in and saw the blood in the tub and the initials HB written on the shower wall with soap. He radioed the station and a detective arrived.

Ryan simply asked the officer to clarify. "So the door was locked when you got there?"

"Yes, Sir. That's why I had to go get the building superintendent."

"Officer, have you worked shooting cases before?"

"Yes, Sir. This is my twelfth shooting case."

"Do people who shoot someone generally turn around and lock the door when they leave?"

The officer looked uncomfortable. "I don't know that I've noticed. I'm not sure."

Under redirect, the prosecutor tried to recover from the officer's testimony. "Is it possible that the door was jammed and not locked?"

The officer looked at the prosecutor and then over to the defense. He knew that he would be recalled if he went with this new theory of the door being jammed. "No ma'am. The door opened too easily once the key was used."

Ryan leaned over and whispered, "Their whole case is falling apart." I nodded.

The detective took the stand. He told of the woman being shot in the head from a gun almost 6 feet away, well out of arms reach of the young lady. He described finding the gun in the tub and that the only fingerprints on it were those of Mr. Bowsman's on the barrel.

The prosecutor smiled as she said to Mr. Ruby, "Your witness."

"The shot came from too far away for Miss Downset to reach by hand?"

"That's correct."

"And how were the fingerprints oriented on the barrel?"

"It was a little weird. They were such that he would have been holding the barrel while it was pointed at himself. I believe he picked it up that way, pulling it out of a bag."

"But you have no proof there was a bag."

"No, but you can't just walk around waving a gun about. You have to put it somewhere."

"So, it could have as easily been pointed at him and he grabbed it, leaving those fingerprints."

"Theoretically."

"Just as your statement about the fingerprints is theoretical."

The prosecutor started to object, but realized it would not go well. The statement could easily be turned into a question that would simply reinforce that there could be alternative theories to the fingerprints.

The next prosecutorial witness was the forensics lab technician. He indicated that the shot went straight through the head just above the bridge of the nose and ended up in the wall behind Miss Downset. The forensics expert again indicated the shot came from beyond Patty's reach and that death was instantaneous.

On cross examination, Mr. Ruby began with a reinforcing question. "So death was instantaneous?"

"Most certainly."

"So, the person couldn't call after being shot?"

"Oh, not at all."

"Or write something?"

"No, Sir."

"Not even with soap?"

"Well, no."

"Let me ask you about the shot and the angle. The shot was from directly in front of her, is that correct?"

"Yes, Sir."

"It wasn't from the side or at an angle?"

"Not at all. From directly in front of her."

"How would Mr. Bowsman get into that position?"

"Well, umm, he'd have to scrunch down and lean across the tub I guess."

"This 5'10" man would have to bend over and twist around over the tub so that he could make that shot?"

"It's the only way he could have done it."

"Not very practical or probably would you say?"

The prosecutor called for an objection. "The defense is asking for conjecture."

Mr. Ruby replied. "Your Honor, I'm pointing out the facts and indicating that the likelihood, as seen by a forensic expert, is not there that a 5'10" man leaned over and twisted himself to make this odd shot."

"Overruled." The judge gaveled.

Mr. Ruby continued. "Did you conduct the subsequent gunpowder residue as requested?"

"I did. We found heavy gunpowder residue along the left foot and toes. Most strange."

"How so?"

"Not the usual place for gunpowder burns."

The prosecutor asked the lab expert if firing near the toes would account for the residue.

"It could, if the foot were being lifted up as the shot was being fired."

Andy Ruby asked a final clarifying question for the lab person. "And if it were a foot coming up, how much space would there be from the foot to the wall?"

The lab expert referred to his report for a moment and then looked up smiling. “There would be 3 inches or less.”

The jury laughed bringing about a reprimand from the judge.

The prosecution brought in a couple more witnesses who said that they had seen Patty and Harold acting as a couple, but nothing directly related to the death. Finally, the prosecution rested.

The judge looked at Mr. Ruby. “The defense will present starting at 9:00 sharp tomorrow. We are in recess until then.” The gavel dropped and the court rose with the judge.

Andy leaned over. “Buck, between you and the yogi providing testimony, I don’t think we will need to put Harold on the stand. I almost think we could rest without any further evidence, but not worth the risk. I’m feeling good.”

The jailers took Harold back and we all left the courtroom. Ms. Alvarez caught Andy as he was walking out.

"Listen, I'm willing to offer your guy a plea bargain. He pleads guilty to manslaughter and does 4 years.”

“We’ll see you tomorrow, Janice.”

"Andy, the deal is off the table tomorrow."

"Janice, the deal is off the table now."

Andy and I walked on out. We could feel the beady eyes trying to burn a hole in our backs. It was not going to be a good week for Ms. Alvarez.

I lost the tie the minute I got in the Jeep. I wasn't sure I would be able to wear one another day or two. It was good to be free of something around my throat. It was a reaction. When I was in the Army, people learned quickly not to grab me around the neck. I almost went into panic mode and people got hurt.

I had once flipped and threw a 230 lbs. karate instructor who was trying to make a surprise demonstration to start a class. He cracked two ribs and had a busted bone in his elbow. Class was over. The adrenaline panic rush made grabbing me near the throat or neck an issue for even the most trained attacker. It was at those times I understood what a berserker really was in combat. Yet there was a time when Trudy could wrap her arms around my neck without triggering the response and later, Dawn could and most recently Kelley.

Once home, I relaxed. I told myself that I could do a week of this if needed. I changed into more comfortable clothes.

Teddy came in. "Hey, Dad! How'd the court thing go?"

"A little better than expected. How was your day?"

"Okay. It looks like Charlie's family has decided to move to North Carolina. She is moving for her Senior year. She's a little bummed out, but her dad already has a job he can transfer to in Wilmington and her mom thinks she can easily find a position as a psychologist in the area, especially with Jacksonville there near the Marine Base."

"Oh. What do you want to do?"

"I just got enrolled for this next year at Eudora High School. If it's okay with you, I'm staying. I'll be heading to UNC after that."

"I'm going to be honest, I'm glad, Son. You know I'll support you going to North Carolina with your mom for high school if you want, but I'm glad you'll be here."

"Thanks, Dad."

Kelley called later that evening. It was about 9:00.

"Buck, I imagine Teddy told you already, but we've decided to move to North Carolina. Victor already has a position in Wilmington. I figure I can open an office there or hire on to a position up by Camp Lejeune. I'd like working with the military. There is a big need for mental health work with combat vets."

"There is. Trudy's family is out there at least half the year. There are plenty of beaches to visit."

"Will you visit?"

"Of course. Teddy will be out there more often I suspect and then there is college."

"I need to talk to Danae."

"She'll understand."

"How was your day in court?"

"It went well. I think the prosecutor is trying to figure a way out of things that will allow her to save face. I don't think it will happen though."

"Are you okay?"

"I get that asked of me a lot lately?"

"But are you?"

"No, but I'll be okay."

"You're honest."

"You know me too well anyway. Wouldn't do any good to lie."

Kelley laughed. "True."

"Good night, Kelley. Sweet dreams."

"You, too, Buck."

Chapter 16: Love Will Keep Us Together

The alarm rang too early for me, but I was supposed to be at court by 9:00. I got up and showered. Coming back to the bedroom to dress, I stared at the tie I had laid out. I wondered if I had a clip-on hidden somewhere. I started looking and then decided this was ridiculous. I didn't mind wearing a nice shirt, slacks, and a jacket, but I needed to draw the line at the tie. They got one day out of me with it, that was enough.

After dressing, I looked in the mirror. Proper society would just have to accept me in an open collar or not at all. The decision itself made me feel better. I still took the Jeep into Kansas City, but I almost opted for the Harley.

I arrived at 8:30 and ran into Andy as we climbed the courthouse steps. He seemed to be in a good mood.

"Good morning, Buck! Ready to testify?"

"When you need me."

We went through security and set up at the defense table. Andy had his files and notes out. Harold was brought in and joined us.

"Good morning, Harold. How are you doing?"

"Honestly, I'll be glad when this is all over, Mr. Ruby."

"I understand. I don't think it will be much longer."

The prosecutor came in. She didn't look very happy. She looked like a whipped pup.

The judge entered and everyone rose. After having everyone sit back down, she turned to the defense table.

"Mr. Ruby, are you ready to proceed?"

"Yes, Your Honor."

Andy called up the Yoga instructor who told about the sessions and the strange request of Patty Downset. I looked at the jury and most of them were nodding as he described developing toe strengthening exercises for the victim.

On cross examination, Miss Alvarez asked the yogi if there were ever any other unusual requests by other patrons that might be similar. The yogi perked up, eager to share.

"Oh, yes. I had one client ask to develop hair muscle exercises."

"Hair muscle?"

"He actually could make his hair stand up at will if it were cut fairly short."

"Did you develop something?"

"I suggested a few things, but there really isn't anything you can do."

"Can you do something for toe muscles?"

"I put some exercises together. Sometimes people like that just want something that they think will help."

"People like what?"

"A bit off balanced. Crazy." The jury laughed which evoked another reprimand from the bench.

"Your Honor," the prosecutor complained, "I'd like to have that last statement struck from the record. The witness is not qualified to judge mental capacity."

The judge looked at the defense. "No objection to striking the statement, Your Honor."

The judge directed the recorder to strike the statement from the testimony. She looked at Mr. Ruby. "Please proceed."

"Your Honor, I'd like to call Buchanan Larson to the stand."

I was sworn in and then sat in the witness chair.

"Mr. Larson, what is your occupation?"

"I'm a private investigator."

"What is your background for investigation?"

"I was trained as a police officer and investigator by the Army. I have worked with police departments and the FBI in solving cases."

"Did you look into this particular case?"

"I did. I was hired by you to look into it."

"What did you find out?"

"It appeared to me almost from the beginning that this was a frame-up for murder. That the actual shooting was done by the victim herself."

"Suicide?"

"Not just suicide. It was an attempt to make the suicide look like a murder."

"Objection!" called the prosecutor. "The victim is not here to defend herself and the witness can't possibly know what was in her mind."

"Your Honor," retorted Mr. Ruby, "the prosecutor has her theory based on the police investigation. My witness, an expert in police investigations, has an alternate theory and one backed by the facts."

"Overruled." The judge dropped the gavel. "Continue Mr. Ruby."

"Would you explain that theory and how it relates to the evidence?"

"The police lab report and the forensic expert actually showed that it was unlikely, even impossible, for Mr. Bowsman to have fired the shot. The angle of the shot was from within the tub space and at a low level."

"What else?"

"The forensic expert indicated that death was instantaneous. There was no way she could have written a possible assailant's initials down after she was shot. It had to be done before."

"That would mean it was a set-up."

"She prepared for some time setting Mr. Bowsman up. She began her intense flexibility and strength training after Mr. Bowsman had indicated he wasn't going to marry her. And she used the fact that he's rather a kind-hearted individual to have him buy her a gun under the ruse that there was a prowler of some sort in the area."

"Then how did she kill herself?"

"She managed to place the .22 automatic between her toes which would be out of reach for her arms. Her flexibility and strength training allowed her to push the trigger with a toe on her right foot. My guess is she observed someone without arms utilize their feet almost as hands at some time, but that part is speculation. No one else could have been in the place where the gun was held. She had been spurned and was trying to get revenge by framing her own suicide as a murder."

"Your Honor, I have already submitted Mr. Larson's report into the record." Andy turned to the prosecutor. "Your witness."

The prosecutor got up, changed her mind, and sat back down. "No, questions, Your Honor."

The judge looked at Mr. Ruby. "Any further witnesses?"

"No, Your Honor."

"How much time do you need for closing?"

"Your Honor, in interest of my client already being held without bond, I'd like to begin now."

"Granted."

Mr. Ruby got up and summarized the case and evidence for the jury. He kept it concise and pointed, indicating the sloppy conclusions of the prosecution team. He finished with a clear, final statement.

"This case should have never gone to trial. The evidence bares this out. Mr. Harold Bowsman is obviously and completely innocent. He should not have even had to spend a single night in jail."

The prosecution closing was very weak. Basically, the argument was that there were two theories presented and that the prosecution thought their case more probable. The appeal was to find some justice for Patty Downset.

The jurors were sent out to deliberate. Harold was moved to a conference room where he sat with Mr. Ruby. I went and got some coffee for the three of us. I just sat down when the bailiff knocked on the door.

"The jury is returning."

Andy looked at me. "It's only been 25 minutes."

"I'm actually surprised it took that long."

We went back into the courtroom and sat at our table. The jury was already in the jury box. When things were settled, the judge re-entered the courtroom to continue the proceedings. She had the defense side stand.

"Mr. Foreman," began the judge. "Did you come to a verdict?"

"We did," offered the foreman. He handed the bailiff the jury form and the judge looked at it. She nodded.

"What say the jury?"

"We find the defendant, Harold Bowsman, not guilty."

Harold began to cry. In his position, I probably would have done the same.

The judge provided the final declaration. "The jury, having found Mr. Bowsman not guilty, is hereby released and this case is closed."

I watched the judge head to her chambers, but she took an evaluative look at the prosecutor. The prosecutor noticed as well. It would take her some time to recover from this disaster.

Harold was shaking hands with friends who were in the gallery. Andy watched him, as did I, revel in his reclaimed freedom.

"Thanks, Buck. You did a great job."

"I appreciate it, Andy. You'll get my bill."

Andy laughed. "It will be worth it. Of course, my client will be the one that pays."

"Need a lift?"

"No. I'll grab a taxi. Thanks, again."

We shook hands and I headed home. This had been an easy case. At least it seemed that way. It was going to be hard to see how the detective agency went now, but we were getting notoriety with our first cases, which ironically would be our last cases, too.

I called Kelley when I got home. I knew she'd want to know that the case was over now and that we had won.

"Kelley?"

"Hi, Buck."

"Are you okay? You sound off."

"My stomach is still bothering me. I've got a doctor's appointment tomorrow. What's up?"

"The case is over. Bowsman was found not guilty."

"Wow! Already? That was fast."

"It was. The prosecution case was really flimsy. Most would never have gone to trial with that evidence."

"I'm glad he won. Any new cases?"

"Not yet. Maybe you should lie down."

"I'm going to. I've been feeling a little tired and nauseated. I'm sure the stress of everything is catching up with me."

"I hope I'm not stressing you."

"You are actually a calming influence. I appreciate that."

"Well, let me know how your doctor's appointment goes. Get some rest."

"Thanks. I will."

A little later Ed called inviting me over to grill out.

"Buck, you need to take a break. Come on up to the house. And bring that young maverick of yours along."

"I'll see if Teddy can join us. I haven't seen him since I got home from court. I'll bring the wine."

"I'll have the steaks."

I texted Teddy to see if he wanted to come with me to Ed's for steak. He was happy to join us, so I texted Ed to let him know. I walked up to the liquor store on Main Street to get some wine for dinner and to stretch my legs. A nice burgundy seemed appropriate for steaks. I'd bring up a bottle of bubbly grape juice so Teddy would have something although he stayed with water a lot these days. I think it was part of his working out with Charlie.

Back home, I put on a pair of walking shorts and pulled out a nice

Guevarra to wear. It was warm and I thought we might be out on the patio.

Teddy came in and when he saw me, he chuckled. "What's up, Magnum?"

"Ha! Ha!"

"Actually, Dad, that might not be a bad look for you."

"Better than my biker jeans and t-shirts?"

"You're right. You'll always be the Biker Dad."

"Thank you. Thank you very much," I said in my best Elvis impersonation.

We walked up to Ed's house carrying our bottles. My wine and Teddy's sparkling grape juice.

"Dad, it's kind of interesting at Charlie's house."

"How so?"

"Well, her parents are trying to get back together, but it seems more awkward there than it has ever been. Everything seems stilted. Like they are trying too hard. Know what I mean?"

"I think so. It's hard, because the potential of a split became very real with the separation, along with the reasons behind the separation. Now it will feel like walking on egg shells, at least for a bit. There's an unconscious fear now of accidentally creating a new split, or a reason to split. It will take some time for things to become more normalized. How's Charlie dealing with it?"

"By leaving the house and working out. Not being home anymore that she has to be. Tonight, she's having dinner with just her mom. I think her parents are really trying to be … well, to connect with the kids."

"It's an interesting situation. When you divorce or separate, or even when there is prolonged tension, many parents will worry that the kids will suffer and try and create strong connections there. If the connections weren't already made, it's not going to go well under stressful times."

"I think she has a strong connection with her mom."

"I do, too."

We got to Ed's. Erin answered the door.

"Well, look at you handsome visitors." She kissed Teddy on his cheek and gave me a hug. "Ed's out back grilling."

“Thanks, Erin. You sure are looking good.”

Erin blushed and then pushed the two of us toward the patio.

“You flirting with my wife, Buck?”

“I sure am, but she says there is only one man for her.”

“I see.” He looked at Teddy. “So when are you running off with my wife?”

Teddy, no stranger to the teasing game, was quick. “As soon as she says she can run off with me.”

We all laughed and then Erin came through the door. We stopped for a moment.

“What did I miss?” she asked accusatorially at us.

The three of us broke out in laughing again. With that, Erin turned around and went back in the house.

Ed started plating the steaks. We all took our steaks medium-rare so they didn’t have to stay on the fire long. With the steaks on a big plate, Erin came out with mashed potatoes and bowls of mixed fruit. It was nice to eat outside.

Erin hadn't forgotten the laughing. "So what was so funny?"

Teddy volunteered to tell her. "They were wondering when you would run off with me."

"Sweetie. I'll run off with you anytime you want."

Ed looked at me. "There you have it. Looks like you and I can do the bachelor thing for the remainder of our days."

Erin playfully slugged him and then gave him a hug.

"Say Buck," Ed got out between a couple bites of steak. "How did your case turn out?"

"Ed, it was the easiest case to solve I've ever seen. I kind of felt sorry for the officer and detective. The prosecutor jumped the gun so bad that it made them all look bad. Very sloppy work."

"So your guy got off?"

"He was found not guilty. We even showed that it was a suicide done up by the girl to make it look like the guy killed her."

"So, will you get paid as well as the last ones?"

"Not as well as the first two cases, but daily expenses and a few incidentals. I still need to submit my bill to the attorney."

"Maybe I should join you. It's got to pay better than Chief of Police here in Eudora."

Erin shook her head. "Now you know you love being the Chief of Police. Plus, you have a nice retirement building. Buck's not going to offer a retirement plan."

I paused in responding. "Hmmm, retirement plan options."

Erin whacked me on the arm. "Stop trying to confuse him, Buck." She turned to Teddy. "How are things going with your girlfriend?"

Teddy told her it all. Planning on going to same college, UNC. Maybe getting a house and living together there in Chapel Hill.

"Well, be sure and be careful and use a condom." Erin's matter-of-fact response left Ed and I looking at her slack jawed. "Oh, come on boys! The times have changed. College kids have sex. I'm glad they're committing to each other."

Teddy laughed. I took a sip of wine. Ed stared at Erin for a minute and then said, "What have you done with my wife?"

The dinner was fantastic. Erin brought out an apple pie for dessert. The four of us had coffee and pie. Erin, who had no qualms about Teddy having sex with his girlfriend, frowned about him drinking coffee. I refrained from saying anything about the odd thinking in that. I could tell Ed was thinking the same thing.

We helped clear the dishes and after we cleaned up, the four of us sat down to play some cards. Fortunately, Teddy knew how to play Pitch, Erin's favorite card game. Teddy and Erin had teamed up against Ed and me. After losing four straight games, I mentioned it was time to head home.

"Can't stand losing, eh?" Erin teased.

"Nope, not at all."

Erin hugged me and then Teddy. Ed walked us to the door.

"Thanks for coming, you two. I appreciate it and Erin needed it."

We walked on home. The Main Street streetlights made it an easy walk and then we cut across Pilla Park to the house.

"That was a fun evening, Dad. I'm going to give Charlie a call before bed. Goodnight."

"Goodnight, Son."

I went upstairs and changed into some pajamas before turning on the late news. There was a small report about Harold being found not guilty. No free publicity for the Morelli and Larson Detective Agency though. I didn't really expect to get that type of coverage in this one.

Kelley called.

"Can you talk, Buck?"

"Sure. Of course I can."

"I didn't wake you, did I?"

"No, Teddy and I just got back from Ed's house. We had dinner there."

"I thought so. Charlie is talking on the phone with Teddy now."

"So what's up?"

"I heard back from the doctor. He knows why I've been tired and my stomach hurt."

"I'm glad he could diagnose it. Did he give you something for it?"

"Oh, it will be better. In a little over 8 more months."

"Huh?"

"I'm pregnant, Buck."

"Wow! And if you are a couple weeks pregnant, then …"

"Yes, you would be the father. Surprise!"

"Are you okay? Well, other than being pregnant?"

"Are you?"

"I am, but I want to know how I can be supportive. Under current circumstances, I'm not sure what to say. I'm excited to have a baby with you, but I don't know how you want to handle this."

"I'm excited and scared at the same time. I want to have the baby. In principle, I think every woman should have the right to choose an abortion, but my choice is to not have one. To keep the baby."

"Thank God. I agree whole-heartedly. It is a woman's choice, but I'm glad you're choosing against it.

I'd support your choice if that was what you wanted, but I'd certainly offer alternatives to look at first."

"Buck, a baby shouldn't be the reason we get together, although I'm sure if it weren't for my marital situation, we would be together regardless of a new baby."

"I agree. So what do you propose?"

"Well, I could try to convince Victor that the baby is his. Well, I could let him assume it is. Just not tell him otherwise."

"I don't think that's good. If you are still planning on giving your marriage a go, starting back up with a lie isn't going to help."

"I'm so glad you said that. I hoped you would say that."

"It's the right thing."

"So that leaves telling him that the baby is yours. Letting him know it was conceived while he and I were legally separated and that I'm going to keep the baby."

"There is one more option. You could come be with me."

"Right after I've committed to try with Victor? We would both know that the baby was the reason. You might never say it. I might never say it. But we'd both know that it was because of the baby. No, I have to try this way. If Victor rejects getting together because of it, then that would be different. I know that doesn't sound fair, but there it is."

"I want you to be happy. So would you acknowledge me as the father? I think I should be able to be a dad to the child."

"I agree. I'm glad you want to. It will be a little Larson."

"This is so messed up. It's like a modern soap opera."

Kelley laughed. "It does seem that way. I wonder what Charlie and Teddy will think when we let them know?"

"That will be interesting. Let me know when you let Charlie know so I can talk to Teddy then."

"I'm going to talk with Victor tomorrow and then I am going to talk to Charlie and Patrick after that. I'll text or call you with an update."

"Thanks."

"Buck?"

"What is it, Kelley?"

"You did want a partnership with me, didn't you?"

"Yes. Not the one I expected, but about this, I'm happy."

"I won't say this to anyone else, but in a way, I am, too."

Epilogue

Kelley called the next day. She said that Victor said he understood and supported her decision. They were still planning on moving to North Carolina by the end of the summer. Kelley promised to provide updates on the baby and include me as much as possible.

When Charlie was told she blurted out that she didn't understand why her mom wasn't with me then. Fortunately, Kelley had talked to the kids alone, so Victor didn't hear the questioning by his daughter. Patrick just thought it was neat and started asking the relationship questions. Kelley explained about being a half-brother or half-sister.

I talked to Teddy who laughed and shook his head. When I asked him about it, he pointed out that when - he didn't say if - he and Charlie got married, the child would be a sibling to both of them. It did make for an odd family tree.

And just to make things odder, Teddy's mom's side of the family lived in Wilmington at least part of the year. At least, that would give Teddy easier access to his new sibling. I knew I'd be visiting Wilmington more.

The thought of getting a beach house in Wrightsville Beach, just outside Wilmington popped into my head. With the trips, it might end up being more cost effective. I probably should just work something out with Trudy's family. They have a guest house on their property in Wilmington. But that thought just seemed too awkward.

The Morelli and Larson Detective Agency became The Larson Detective Agency. I got plenty of calls. Most of the work was minor detective work. Following up on potential affairs or insurance scams. I declined most of them. I'd probably regret it later but my heart wasn't in that kind of work right then.

Trudy had called not long after I told Teddy. I never told him to keep it a secret from his mom. I never thought that was a good idea to have a child keep a parent's secret from the other parent except when it was a gift or something to be a surprise. She actually listened and I never heard judgment about the situation. She was curious about how the logistics would work and she admitted she was a little bit pleased that Teddy would be out to North Carolina a little more, but she did offer to help. I think she would have genuinely meant it except it would involve her parents some.

Teddy would be going to Eudora High School here his Senior year. Charlie would be transferring to E.A. Laney High School in Wilmington. I pointed out to her that Laney was where Michael Jordan had gone to high school. She looked pleasantly surprised.

I'm here. Here in Eudora. Finding life can be very strange and knowing that when it comes to romance, I'm not a lucky person. But for the first time in a long while I realized; I'm not unlucky in it either.

Character List from Previous Books

Buchanan "Buck" Henry Larson

Trudy Ryan Larson, Buck's ex-wife

Theodore "Teddy" Larson, Buck's son

Kelley Morgan, Ph.D., psychologist

Danae Cornwall, Ph.D., Kelley Morgan's partner in therapy office

Charlotte "Charlie" Morgan, daughter of Dr. Kelley Morgan

Christina "Tina" Thomas, secretary

James Gilliford, attorney and Dr. Cornwall's boyfriend

Ed Hatfield, Eudora Chief of Police

Erin Hatfield, wife of Ed Hatfield

Book 1: It's Not the Destination; It's the Ride

Sharon Waters, missing girl

Timmy Waters, brother of Sharon Waters

Julie Kraven, friend of Sharon Waters

Dawn Stevens, Posey County Sheriff Deputy and Buck's deceased

Girlfriend

Father Pete Callihan, Holy Family Catholic Church priest

Roy Bean, Carmi Police Detective

Alvin Baker, Carmi Police Detective

Todd Jenkins, Eudora High School student

Edgar Bathrick, murderer of Dawn Stevens

Brittany Smythe, Edgar Bathrick dinner date.

Theresa Bender, friend of Dawn Stevens

Freddy Erickson, husband of Theresa Bender

Charlotte Colcade, friend of Dawn Stevens

Charles Colcade, husband of Charlotte Colcade

Richard "Dick" Mason, Mt. Vernon Police Officer

Randy Kowlzski, bartender at American Legion

Veronica Tate, Eudora High student who committed suicide

Don Francis, Eudora High Principal

James (Jim) Thibold, Eudora Schools Superintendent

Jeremy Martinez, one of Buck’s soldiers who died

Karen Gold Martinez, wife of Jeremy Martinez

Nicolette “Nici” Martinez, daughter of Jeremy and Karen Martinez

Thom Magnus, Pastor of Heaven’s Crest Baptist Church

Tim Marquette, employee at Evansville’s Harley-Davidson shop

Thelma Bleaker, cashier at Two Tony’s Restaurant

Samuel “Sam” John Waters, Sharon Water’s father

Laverne Waters, wife of Sam Waters

Cali MacKenzie, girlfriend of Timmy Waters

Scott MacKenzie, pastor in Carmi

Ann MacKenzie, wife of Scott MacKenzie

Conner Perkins, Julie Kraven’s boyfriend

Stanley Timmons, busboy at Two Tony’s Restaurant

June Kraven, mother of Julie Kraven

Jasmin Ramirez, waitress at Jasmin Restaurant

Jackie McFadden, Steven's family attorney

A.C. Monroe, Hopkinsville news reporter

Irving Timmons, father of Stanley Timmons

Timothy September, childhood friend of Buck Larson

Rodrigo Vargas, Costilla County Deputy Sheriff

Hector Gallo, boy who stole a car

Jimmy Young, boy who stole a car

Martha Young, mother of Jimmy Young

Book 2: Live to Ride and Ride to Live

Tim Dossett, Topeka Chief of Police

Teri Anne Prickles, shooting victim

John Howard Prickles, husband of Teri Anne Prickles

Norma Jean Battes, shooting victim

Christopher "Chris" Battes, husband of Norma Jean Battes

Wanda Howard, shooting victim

Fred Howard, husband of Wanda Howard

Griffin Ford, Sergeant with KBI

Delores Jenkins, FBI profiler

Victor Morgan, husband of Dr. Kelley Morgan

Patrick "Pat" Morgan, son of Dr. Kelley Morgan

Helen Danford, shooting victim

Howard Danford, husband of Helen Danford

John Redhawk, Ph.D., professor at HINU

Floyd Ramsey, Adjutant General of Kansas National Guard

Debbie Allen, shooting victim

Kirby Allen, husband of Debbie Allen

Book 3: En Mi Viejo San Juan

Raul Cuzo, friend of Buck Larson

Anthony Wiggins, Mayor of Mt. Vernon

Bud Cox, Councilman

Jerry Cross, Councilman

Linda Means, Councilwoman

Melanie "Mel" Louis, conference attendee in Puerto Rico

Nina Mercedes de Cuzo, wife of Raul Cuzo

Marquita Cuzo-Mercedes, daughter of Raul Cuzo

Luisa Cuzo-Mercedes, daughter of Raul Cuzo

Charles Louis, husband of Melanie Louis

Emilia "Emi" Reyes, murder victim in Panama

Juan Lopez, citizen of Santa Barbara

Gabriel Rodriguez, citizen of Santa Barbara

Erica Louis, daughter of Melanie Louis

Grayson Louis, son of Melanie Louis

Elmer "Elmo" P. Elmhurst, Esq., drug smuggler

Kipp Fearing, FBI agent

Beth McFadden, daughter of Jackie McFadden

Daniel Hennesey, DEA agent

James Talbert, FBI agent

Marques Fields, FBI agent

Rachel Jenkins, reporter and cousin of Delores Jenkins

Book 4: Panheads, Knuckleheads and Other Things That Bang

Leslie Fearing, brother of Kipp Fearing

Eugene Wallace, LTC(R), former Provost Marshall

Kevin Gorman, President of Oz HOGs

Terry Roe, secretary applicant

Evette Monteski, secretary applicant

Linda Vector, secretary applicant

Chauncy Harper, client of Dr. Morgan and boyfriend of Trudy

Larson

David Hickman, former MP, missionary

Agnes McEwan, sister of Ed Hatfield

Norman Tate, father of Victoria Tate

Debbie Tate, mother of Victoria Tate

Danny Evergreen, boyfriend of Victoria Tate

Ramona Tensley, client of Dr. Morgan

Made in the USA
Middletown, DE
13 July 2023

34996504R00189